The Wish That Saved Christmas

A Heart-warming Festive Adventure

Kate A. Harvey

ISBN 13: 978-1-7395507-1-4

Cover design and illustrations by: Kate Harvey

Produced in the United Kingdom

www.kate-harvey.co.uk

For Grace

CHAPTER 1

NELL'S AWAKENING

Colourful lights filled the sky, their promise of hope twinkling in Nell's eyes. Soon they would shine even brighter. Her head poked out of the breast pocket of Emma's red woolly coat as she stomped along the frosty pavement with her mother. Nell didn't mind being jostled; she knew it was only because Emma was so upset. Nell herself couldn't move at all, of course not. What would you expect from a tiny painted figurine usually kept on a shelf?

'They say it's beautiful,' said Emma's mother looking up at the colour speckled clouds. 'It's a lovely idea from the mayor, isn't it, for everyone to bring a decoration for the giant Christmas tree in the square? A good way to keep our spirits up until they cure the horrible illness. I am so proud of this town!'

'Dad can't see it, though, can he?' Emma frowned as she kicked a stone along the path. She missed her father, who was in the hospital, unable to move or speak. He had caught the strange new sickness with hundreds of others, leaving their families and the whole town in chaos. 'And anyway, we are leaving Hope's End before Christmas, so it doesn't even count.' Emma huffed and shook her head. 'There had better be an angel on that tree.'

Nell thought of Emma before everything changed, telling terrible jokes, and laughing, baking cookies, and reading books, and climbing trees with her friends. Now she was sad and moody most of the time. Seeing her like this was unbearable. Nell sent Emma wisps of comforting thoughts. Perhaps seeing the gigantic Christmas tree would cheer her up.

'There might be an angel. Or a star perhaps,' said her mother. 'Everyone is bringing something special. Our star garland will look lovely up there, won't it? And I don't mind having to leave it behind when we go. It's a gift to the town.' She smiled, though it didn't quite reach her eyes. 'Almost there.'

They walked down Church Street, past the boarded-up shops and piles of uncollected rubbish bags to Riverside Square. Their cheeks stung in the chill of the wind; their breath danced in front of them. Of course, Nell's tiny body could not feel the cold. Emma stopped grumbling only as they turned through the gap in the yew hedge. They stopped in their tracks.

Emma gaped up at the largest and most beautiful

Christmas tree she had ever seen. Nell wobbled in the pocket as Emma's heart thumped. They stood, dazzled by the glitter and shimmer of the gigantic pine tree that towered as high as the church spire behind. Its vast sweeping branches groaned with the festive belongings of the people of Hope's End. Thousands of glittering decorations twisted in the wind. Lights in every colour of the universe. Baubles and garlands, curiosities, and treasures. A tree filled with last-chance hope.

People crowded in the square for the first time all year: sisters, brothers, uncles, aunts, children, grandparents, daughters, and sons. Tables, ladders, and whirring cranes filled the space, with people bustling around them. Collection boxes for food, gifts, and other donations lined the riverside railings. Dozens of eyes cast upwards, glinting in the lights at the glorious tree, hopeful offerings clutched in hands. Last attempts to end the terrible illness that caused so much suffering. The scent of pine and cinnamon curled around them. The mayor, a stout woman with spiky hair and a red dress, stood on a box ready to make a speech. She wore an enormous colourful jewelled collar, which glinted in the lights of the tree. Nell thought she looked like a human Christmas decoration, though she didn't like to judge. Emma rolled her eyes as the mayor put her glasses on, pulled out a piece of paper and began.

'In these dark days, as this terrible year draws to a close, we, the people of Hope's End, can only hope for a brighter future. This crisis has stretched our town to its limits. What holds us together is our unity, our love, hope, and community–'

One of Emma's friends on the opposite side of the square admired the tree with her dad. He was holding her close to him with her mother on the other side. A fire of jealousy streaked through Emma, a tear forming in the corner of her eye. Nell knew exactly how she was feeling and wished she could bring Emma's father home, to give Emma's mother back her job. To make everything right again. The tear splashed from Emma's eye onto Nell's head. Nell sent soothing thoughts to Emma, hoping she would feel less alone. She felt her relax a little, her breath steady. The mayor continued.

'On this mid-winter day, we transform our famous great pine tree in Riverside Square into an enormous Christmas tree, filled with our favourite treasures, decorations, curiosities, and symbols of hope. I have lent my cherished angel for the treetop. Isn't she beautiful? I always thought she might be real, ha ha!' She smiled and shook her head.

'Hope so!' shouted a man.

'We need it!' said another. The mayor adjusted her glasses.

'Our Christmas tree creation will stir hearts and souls and inspire us to find a way, together, through these troublesome times. When this is over, our town will be restored to its former glory. Our favourite shops will re-open, our award-winning school will have teachers again, and our people will be healthy and happy. We will thrive once more if we all pull together and resolve this mystery sickness.'

'Isn't it fabulous!' said Emma's mother. 'All the

lovely people of this wonderful town coming together, even in hard times!' She waved across the square to some other parents.

'All the lovely people we will never see again because we have to move,' said Emma. Her mother's shoulders dropped at little. She had dark circles under her eyes.

'I am sorry darling, it's just the way it is.'

Emma placed her hand to her chest, against the breast pocket where Nell stood. Ahead, a woman stood on a crane holding a magnificent angel aloft. Emma's eyes lit up. If you looked closely, so did Nell's. The people cheered as the woman rose on the crane and attached the angel to the treetop. Gold and glinting against the lights, the angel towered over them all. Her elegant, pointed wings seemed to pierce the swirling green tinged clouds above. She swayed in the breeze, back and forth, back, and forth. A group of crows swooped low across the square, cawing. Some people drew their small children close.

A woman with heavy eyelashes holding something blue and glittery in her hand swiped them away.

'Hey!' she yelled, 'someone bring some bird killer!'

'That's cruel,' said Emma. The mayor continued.

'Our hearts go out to those in hospital, those who have lost their jobs and homes. Please make donations for those in need in the boxes – your spare food, clothes, money, and toys are appreciated. And please take what you need. We will gather here on Christmas morning to give out donated gifts and to reflect. By supporting each other, we will beat this menace! Merry Christmas!'

Emma handed the star garland they had brought from home to a man with a pile of Christmas decorations in his arms. He took it and smiled.

'Thanks, love, enough stars in your home already, are there?' He nudged her arm. 'That's a pretty one!' He climbed up a very tall ladder that leant against the tree and added it with the new decorations to the masterpiece. Nell's eyes twinkled.

*

Nell usually stood on the shelf by Emma's bed with her other treasures. She was a gift from Emma's great-grandmother when she was younger. '*Keep her close, dear,*' Emma's great-grandmother had said, with a wink. Emma had done exactly that. Nell stood next to a photo of her father, who was grinning at a tomato for some reason; half a fossil she had found on a beach and a grubby duck teddy she adored when she was a baby. Nell stood in the middle, with her two long plaits and her red jumper, with little blue forget-me-not flowers painted on the front.

When Emma's father went to the hospital earlier in the year, Emma took Nell from the shelf and carried her with her in her pocket. Since her mother lost her job, she sneaked her to school inside her rucksack every day. When she heard that they might have to move to the next town, Pewksbury, she slept with her under her pillow at night. Of course, Emma did not know that Nell could think and feel. How could she? Nell never moved or spoke, just like any ordinary figurine. But she was right there by her side, alright. Especially in dark times like these. No. Questions. Asked.

'Do you think it's a real angel, Mum?' asked Emma.

'I am not sure, darling.' She shifted uneasily.

'I believe it's real,' said Emma, crossing her arms. 'Otherwise, everything is just too awful. Why can't you adults just sort out these problems? We need an angel. Something good has to happen.'

A wide man moved in front of them, blocking their view. He smelt of old socks mixed with pubs and pie. He looked up at the angel and sniggered. Emma's mother tapped him on the shoulder, and he turned around. His shiny cheeks drooped down to his chin and his tiny eyes were almost buried beneath his floppy eyebrows. Even before he spoke, Nell knew who it was. Emma grimaced and folded her arms even tighter.

'Such a pity!' he purred, placing his clammy hand on Emma's mother's arm. His eyes narrowed further into the folds of his face as he attempted a false smile.

'Mr Tribulus, hello. I hoped we might see you. You see, I was wondering if you might change your mind.' She clasped her hands together. 'It is a lot to ask, I know. I am certain I will have some money to pay you for the rent soon, just not right now. Since you doubled it when I lost my job, and with my husband in the hospital, well, it's hard. We really would like to stay. Perhaps I could work in one of your many businesses here? Please?' Nell felt Emma cringe. Mr Tribulus shook his head. Sweat flew off him and landed on her forehead. Warm air blasted over Nell as Emma huffed through her nostrils and wiped it off.

'I am afraid there is simply nothing I can do.' His thin mouth almost disappeared out of sight into his fleshy chin. Which was fortunate because he had a large piece of gristle stuck between his teeth.

'Slug,' muttered Emma. Nell slipped down a little as Emma's mother elbowed her.

'Well, Mr Tribulus, here is my card.' She tried to meet his eyes and handed it to him with her own best attempt at a smile. She grasped her hands together again. 'If you can think of anything. Any way to allow us to pay the rent a little later. Or work here in Hope's End. Please. Anything.' Nell knew Emma's stomach was churning. It was so humiliating.

'Goodbye, Susan. You can drop the keys in to me at Gluttontwerp House by the end of Christmas Eve. Three days is very generous, I think you will agree.'

'My name is Sara,' she croaked. He looked up at the tree again, laughed and shook his head. He blustered off, shedding beads of grease, and muttering to himself as he walked.

Emma's mother put her purse and remaining cards back into her handbag and pretended she wasn't crying. 'Well, that's fine! Good actually! I love Pewksbury anyway, always wanted to live there. There's a lovely view of the sewage works from the flat. And I'm sure I will enjoy working at that new factory. I've never worked with experimental

chemicals before. We will get used to the smells.'
Nell sensed Emma's heart clenching.

'I thought you said it was a sherbet factory?' said
Emma.

'Oh, did I? Well, there really is very little
difference.' She squirmed.

'I would rather starve to death than live there. I.
Am. Not. Going.' Emma re-crossed her arms. If she
had more arms to cross, she would have. 'We belong
here, and that's that.'

'And did you know Pewksbury school has
reopened since the enquiry into the dead fish?'

But Emma wasn't listening. As the mayor gazed
up at her glinting angel high above, the greatest idea
she ever had bubbled into her mind. An idea that
would change everything. Emma turned away from
her mother and pressed her hands against her chest,
squashing Nell closer to her heart. Nell followed her
gaze up – to the angel at the top of the tree. Emma
spoke in a tone you might use to address royalty.

'Oh, Angelic One. I absolutely and completely
know you are real. I believe! So please grant my wish.
Stop Mr Tribulus from being such a greedy, vile,
slug-headed twit. I don't want to live in pukey
Pewksbury, I want to stay here in Hope's End. Please
make Dad better and give Mum back her job. She
loved working at the bookshop. Please, only you can
help me. Thank you.' She bowed her head, her eyes
shut so tight that her face scrunched up. The angel
stared down at them, swaying to and fro, gleaming
against the inky, greenish sky.

At the very moment Emma made her wish, Nell's

body fizzed and popped all over. It tingled and prickled in her core and sparkled and buzzed on her edges. Feelings she had never had before. It was as if starlight swirled through her, into every particle. Her soul shone. A faint beat in her chest grew strong, pulsing and thumping. Energy whizzed from the top of her little head to the tips of her tiny toes. She wriggled them. She stared at her fingers and opened and closed her hands.

'Blinking baubles, I can move!' said Nell. She put her hand to her mouth and pressed it. 'And I can speak! What's happening to me?' She wriggled some more, delight fizzing through her. She laughed, a little too loud, then stopped herself and covered her mouth with her hands again. 'Oops!' She looked up at Emma from the pocket and stood still.

'What's so funny?' said Emma and her mother at the same time, looking at each other. 'Nothing,' they both said. They each thought the other had finally cracked up.

Nell sank into the pocket, holding her hands over her smiling mouth. She squeezed her eyes shut as if to hold in the beautiful new feelings of life that whirled wildly inside. She didn't know what to think about first, or what to do. So, she stayed still and quiet. One powerful thought would not leave her. Emma had wished on the angel, and Nell would do everything she could to make sure the angel got that wish. It was their only hope. She gazed up at the angel, courage blazing in her heart. I am coming to have a word with you! They turned to go home.

CHAPTER 2

THE GIGANTIC CHRISTMAS TREE

Nell tumbled out through the letterbox of 25a Oakwood Road at five minutes past midnight, excitement tingling through her. She hit the ground, hard.

'Ow!' She stood up and dusted herself off. The rainbow of lights from the Christmas tree danced against the clouds to the north side of Hope's End. Emma and her mother snored inside. She hurried along the icy pavement towards the lights. She smiled at the pat-pat of her own tiny feet sounding in her ears. Her mission flashed inside her like a beacon. To the angel. Her stomach clenched as she remembered what Mr Tribulus had said. How could he kick them out of their home three days before

Christmas? Emma was right. He was an evil, slug-headed, greedy twit. She ran past the rats squeaking from the drains beneath. Under the abandoned car. Past the bones of a long dead small animal. The whispering dark winds swirled damp, mouldy leaves into her face. She threw them aside.

A crow's caw cracked through the still air. She froze as it drew closer. His jagged black wingtip caught her as he swooped and knocked her over with a thud.

'Hey!' she said. 'Watch where you're going!' He cawed in her face as he passed and flapped away into the dark night. She huffed, brushed herself off again, and sped towards the lights.

She squeezed under the hedge stuffed with litter and hurried through a garden. She skipped over the snowdrop shoots and slid over a frozen pond. Beneath the ice, three goldfish swam in the near-freezing water. She glided across, laughing, and spinning to the other side. Straight into two large, glaring eyes. Oops! A mangy fox with slits in both ears towered above her. He breathed his musty breath over her. She wrinkled her nose. A menacing scar across his forehead twitched as he narrowed his eyes and hissed in her face. She blinked, then held his gaze, and put her hands on her hips.

'Do you mind? You are in my way!' she said and stuck her tongue out at him. Confusion flashed across his eyes, and he stepped back. Ducking under him, she hurried onwards, following the light reflections in the clouds.

She remembered Emma's face, wet with tears, as

she threw her belongings in the packing boxes earlier, ready for the move. Her chest ached. She thought of Emma's mother's weak smile as she told her everything was going to be fine, even though they all knew that it wasn't. She rushed alongside the familiar tall yew hedge, studded with its jewel-red berries, to the gap up ahead. Almost there. Through the gap, frosty cobbles glinted with colourful light from the tree. She turned in and caught her breath. Her mouth gaped open at the sight of it. She stopped. It took her breath away.

'Blinking baubles,' she said. The cranes, ladders, tables, and people that filled the square earlier had gone. The Christmas trees' vast branches rippled in the crisp breeze, sending baubles spinning and garlands swinging. Nell's eyes followed all the way to the top. Her core flickered at the sight of the angel, who stared out into the dark, moonless sky. She swayed in the wind, her long wings stretching high. Nell sighed. The angel would make things well again. She knew it, just like Emma did. She just had to make sure she answered the wish. Only the small matter of reaching her. Dozens of metres up through a gigantic Christmas tree. That's all. Nell smiled to herself and nodded. Oh, and back home again. Easy! She breathed a heavy breath out and set off across the colour specked cobbles towards the shimmering masterpiece, her plaits flapping about behind her. *I will be back soon, Emma!*

Two crows quarrelled on the railings by the river to the right of the square. They stopped, startled to see the tiny figure race across to the tree. The boats on the river knocked together, bobbing on the silver night-water. A light was on in one of the boats, where a woman sat reading and eating something. The smell of mince pies wafted out over the square, filling Nell with sweetness as she ran. To the left, a man slept on a bench. An old newspaper flapped over his face as he snored. Nell stopped by a woodlouse who lay upside down on the ground. She helped him over, then waved at him as he scurried away.

She skidded to a stop in front of the tree, its enormous limbs looming over her, hiding the angel from view. The star garland Emma and her mother had brought twirled high above, nestled amongst the other hopeful belongings. She took a deep breath and searched for a way up.

CHAPTER 3

PICK ON SOMEONE YOUR OWN SIZE

Nell tiptoed into the dark emptiness underneath the sprawling branches. Rustling and clicking sounds filled the cool air. Those eerie, unnamed noises that only come at night. It smelt damp and earthy. An icy shiver rippled through her. She pulled her arms around herself and ran towards the trunk. Dead pine needles crunched under her feet. She placed her hand against the coarse bark of the vast trunk and patted it. It was far too wide to climb. Nell looked up through the hundreds of limbs and branches that disappeared into the distant heights like a brown skeleton. She heard a rat squeak. If there was ever a place that you might get eaten alive, this was it. Given that she had only just come to life, she wasn't about to let that happen. The first branch towered high above her like a thick arm pointing back towards the town. She shuddered, then hurried back to the front of the tree. She breathed in the scent of cinnamon mingled with pine that hung like a mist. The sparkling branches creaked above her. Just as a twist of worry arose in her belly, there was a sound from above.

'Pssst.' A voice came from near the end of the lowest branch that hung above her. Startled, she jumped.

'What the–' she said. She craned her neck and squinted up. Beyond the dazzle of the fairy lights, something moved. The pine needles rustled. A face no bigger than hers emerged from between the deep green fronds and peered through the needles at her. She straightened up and cocked her head. Another appeared, and another. One– two– three– eight tiny wooden faces gaped down at her. Her mouth dropped open; she hadn't expected company.

'Pssst,' came the voice again. Nell waved.

'Hello!' she said. Eight little hands waved back. They were a group of miniature musicians, with cheerful round faces, smiling eyes, and rosy cheeks. As small as your thumb, they seemed old-fashioned, wearing glossy black coats with gold buttons. Their matching hats had gold loops sticking out of the top. Each held a musical instrument or songbook in their little wooden hands. Her eyes lit up.

'Who are you?' said one, eyeing her.

'I'm Nell,' she said, twirling her plait around her

hand.

'Why are you lurking and scurrying about down there?' The little person waved a rod with a lighted star at the end.

'I'm not doing it on purpose. I want to get up on the tree.' She squinched her eyes to see better. Although theirs was the lowest branch, it was still impossible to reach. 'I am going to the top. I have to meet the angel.' She pointed up; her body tightening as she waited for their reply. 'I am on a mission to save my human,' she added with a firm nod.

'A mission?' Their faces disappeared into the branches, whispering to each other. She crossed her fingers behind her back. After a moment, the eight beaming faces pushed back through the needles.

'How about we throw this down–' He wobbled a fairy light wire, so it shook. 'And you can climb up?'

'Yes, please!' Nell squeezed her palms together, excitement bubbling inside.

'Oi!' came a voice from above the wobbling lights. 'Do you mind?'

'Alright, keep your hair on!' He glanced up and then back to Nell, rolling his eyes.

'Hold on tight everyone!' He used his staff to push the lights off the end of their branch. They each clutched the pine fronds as the entire thing pinged up, then bounced back into place. The lights flopped down, although not close enough.

'Careful! Hold on!' he said. The lights caused the branch above to rock.

'Oi!' came another voice. 'Some of us are trying to sleep.' Nell's wide eyes peered up but couldn't see anyone. Were there many more beings like her?

'How about a bit of community spirit?' said the little man. 'She is on a mission, for goodness' sake.' He waved towards Nell, then looked up, his hands on his hips. 'Well, let's get to work!' He clapped his hands and rubbed them together. 'A friend in need is a friend indeed.' Nell blushed. A friend? The string of lights dropped again, dangling to the ground next to Nell.

'Thank you!' She smiled and clambered on pulling herself up with her own arms, like when Emma climbed trees in the park. She watched her hands clasp the lights string one after the other, working with her feet to pull herself up. It was difficult to stop herself squealing with joy, but she did; she wanted to make a good impression. Eyes and whisperers watched her through the bottom of the sweeping branch. As she climbed, a crow eyed her from across the square, slowly flapping his wings. She picked up her pace.

Above her stretched branch after branch, dripping with treasures. Shining baubles in all different shapes and sizes. Glass icicles glinted against the coloured lights. A small violin hovered above her, playing music by itself. It wasn't only Christmas decorations; other interesting belongings caught her eye as she climbed. A copper kaleidoscope with a spinning glass barrel on one end filled with coloured beads and stones. There was a model of a red post-box turning in the breeze. It coughed, sending a letter flying out of its slot and into Nell's face. She laughed awkwardly and continued. A sloth decoration wearing a red hat hung upside down from the branch. Was that a yawn? Next to it hung a small wind-up music box with all the workings visible. Wonder swelled inside her like a balloon. A shining lizard with petrol colours darted over it and dived into a little red stocking. Startled, Nell caught her breath and carried on. It was hard to focus on climbing. She wished she had more eyes so she could see everything at once. Something like a firefly buzzed around her face, which didn't help. She swatted around her head until it flew off.

As she drew close to the branch, her attention turned to the little singers who waited for her in a moon shape on the branch. Eight sets of intelligent eyes gazed at her above the spiky pine needles. The smallest singer jumped up and down, grinning. They reached out to her with their tiny hands, smiling encouragement to her. She reached towards them, just as a dark expression crossed their faces. Their smiles wiped away; their eyes filled with white as they fixed on something behind her. She spun around to see what it was and stared right into the eyes of another crow. Her body froze in fear though she tried to scramble away, her limbs quaking, her breath short. He opened his powerful black beak and closed it around her little body, plucking her out. The singers gasped and held their hands to their faces. She thrashed around to break free, but the crow gripped tighter and flew higher. She let out a howl of terror.

'Put me down!' She thumped at him. 'Pick on someone your own size!' Determined as she was, dread swept through her. He flapped higher and higher, taking her away from the choir, who gaped helplessly up at them. She wriggled, but it didn't help. The crow flew two branches up with Nell clasped in his beak.

'Nell!' they cried. 'Help! Save her!'

A thick pine needle arrow arched out from between the branches far above her, striking the crow between the eyes. Dazed, he opened his beak, releasing Nell, who fell flat on her face on the nearest branch with a bounce. The crow flew off and settled itself on the railings by the river.

Nell's head spun. She shook herself and blinked several times before she gathered her senses. She sat up on the branch. There were no lights or decorations, and the needles were brown. She looked up to see who had shot the arrow. There was no-one there. She was far above the choir, alone again. A chill crept through her as the needles further along the bleak branch rustled. A shadowy figure emerged, a little taller than her. Nell stood up.

'Oh, I am sorry if I disturbed you,' she said, her body tense.

'No matter.' His voice grated in her ears. He slinked out of the gloom and into a patch of light near Nell. Tall and thin, his face formed a sour point, crackled, and covered in bumps. He had a pointed beard, an old crown, and a flaking cloak the colour of a gravestone at night. His eyes were deep set, like black holes. They locked onto Nell's.

'Nice of you to drop in. Heh, heh.' A shadow crossed his stony face.

'Ha,' said Nell, though she didn't think it was funny. She still felt stunned. He walked over to her and stared right into her eyes. Her stomach knotted.

'You're new?' His eyes flickered as he stepped closer. Nell forced a smile. She knew it's often better to be polite, though she moved back from him.

'Oh, yes, I am. How did you–?'

'I can sense these things. Did your human bring you?' He strolled around her in a circle, inspecting her. She pulled her arms around herself.

'No, I, I brought myself. I'm here to speak to the angel.' She stiffened, wishing that she hadn't told him.

'An imposter! Ha ha.' He nudged her with his elbow and smiled a wintry smile. 'Only joking.' He looked up. 'You think an angel will speak to you?' He smirked, showing perfect yellow teeth. 'What's your name?'

'Nell,' she said. He peered into her eyes again. The flicker inside her heart died down a little.

'Interesting.' He nodded. She looked away and searched for a way down to her friendly singers, breathing fast. The figure turned to face the centre of the tree and wandered towards it. 'And very funny! You, speak to an angel! Anyway, things to do. It was nice to meet you, Nell. I'm sure we will meet again!' He waved over his shoulder, still sniggering, and stalked back into the darkness. A black, bony beetle she didn't notice at first seemed to follow behind him.

'Goodbye.' Her voice wavered. The singers shouted up to her from far below.

'Hey, Nell, Nell! Are you there?' Nell put her hand to her chest and breathed deeply. Her shoulders relaxed a little, though she was shaking. She looked up. She could continue to the angel since she was a little further up. Though perhaps reaching her wasn't going to be easy after all. The top seemed even further away, hidden in cloud. The ground was now far below. The musician had called her a friend. She thought of Emma, her struggling family, awful Pewksbury and greedy Mr Tribulus. Failing didn't bear thinking about. The wish had to come true. She found a long wide ribbon, tugged it to test its strength, and slid down to them. They had helped her once. Perhaps she might need them again.

CHAPTER 4

NUMINKIND

'What an entrance, Nell! Ha! Very impressive!' The little man slapped his thigh. 'Are you alright? Come and sit with us!' He beckoned her over with his staff. The star on its end glowed warm-white.

'Yes, fine now, thank you. Hello!' Coming down was easier than climbing up, and more fun. Her chest lifted at the sight of them, and she flopped onto a nearby glittering toadstool.

'Ow!' it said and shoved her off. It hobbled away and turned its back to them.

'Oh, I'm sorry, I didn't realise you were, ahem. Sorry.' It was hard to know what was living and what wasn't. She blushed and moved to sit on the branch, smoothing the needles flat first.

'So, Nell, you know to watch out for those crows

now, I see, ha! We aren't sure what's going on with them. Got out of the wrong side of bed, eh? Now, tell me, you say you seek the angel?' The tiny man tapped his finger against his chin and walked along the middle of the branch with an air of expectation.

'Yes. I'm on my way to make sure Emma's wish comes true.' She filled with pride as she heard herself say it out loud. 'Who are you?' She settled her hands into her lap, her tension draining away. The little man puffed out his chest. The others copied.

'We are the Hawthorn House Miniature Choir, on a mission of hope, like all the others.' He waved vaguely around the tree. They each saluted. Nell saluted back. 'Here for our humans, and our poor, tragic town.' He shook his head and sighed. 'Terrible times.' He held out his hand to her. 'Opus.' He smiled.

'Pleased to meet you!' Nell shook it and smiled back.

'Poco!' The smallest one bounced over to her, his eyes shining. 'Great to meet you! Really, really great!' He shook her hand in both of his, jerking Nell's arms. The others jostled each other out of the way to introduce themselves. She couldn't hear all their names because they all spoke at once. Nell shook hands with each of them, soaking in their joyful spirits. Each had a face like a circle of kindness.

'So, Nell, tell us about this wish to the angel; your mission?' Opus twirled his hand, gesturing for her to continue.

'Well, Mr Tribulus, who is horrible, by the way, told Emma's mother they have to leave their home.

They can't pay him money for the rent. So, they must move to Pewksbury by the end of Christmas Eve. Emma has lived in this town all her life and doesn't want to leave.' She opened her arms out. 'Her friends are here, her home, her school, her everything!'

'Oh, dear. Not Pewksbury!' The singers shuffled and spoke in low voices to each other, shaking their heads and wrinkling their noses.

'That's the worse place this side of–' began Poco, before another nudged him to be quiet. Nell shifted nervously.

'He won't wait!' She flung her arms even wider. 'She hoped to find a new job, but there aren't any. Most of the shops and businesses have closed. The school has no teachers. Emma's father is very ill in hospital. He has been there all year with hundreds of others. So, he can't help.' She shrugged.

'I am sorry to hear it,' said Opus. 'This town is in terrible trouble. One day, everything was fine, the next, poof! People are conking out all over the place and everything stopped. They never visit our Hawthorn House anymore.' His voice wavered. 'Poco's plans to build an obstacle course are crushed.'

'The House is incredibly boring, Nell, I just wanted to spice things up,' Poco said, huffing.

'Well, Emma made this wish to the angel. To stop Mr Slug, I mean, Mr Tribulus, so we can stay. We have had enough.' She put her hands on her hips.

'Quite. And Pewksbury is dreadful, always was. It's not their fault of course. The sewage works are the highlight of the town. Oh, it's nothing like this sparky place. And this Tribulus is making them leave? At Christmas?' He curled his lip in disgust.

'Yes!' Her eyes brightened; she was glad to be understood. The group murmured rude words about Mr Tribulus to each other, shaking their heads. Poco kicked a bauble so hard that he stubbed his toe and hopped around on the branch in circles, clutching his foot.

'Oh, are you alright?' asked Nell, getting up. Poco nodded through a stiff smile, still holding his foot.

'Fine! Really, it's nothing!'

'Anyway, he is a slug. Although that is insulting to slugs. And he's rich. He could easily wait, give Emma's mum a chance to find some money. He owns lots of businesses, including a new plastic company. The type of plastic that makes getting toys out of packets really hard!'

'Sounds like a right twit!' called Poco. Now that he had recovered from his stubbed toe, he stamped his other foot, hard.

'Yes, so, I'm travelling to the top to make sure the angel got the wish and get home before Emma wakes up.' Nerves twisted in her tummy as she looked up. All she could see was layer upon layer of pine needles, and baubles gently swaying, those strange, greenish clouds floating in the dark sky high above.

'Nell, my dear, this isn't an ordinary tree. Even getting to the top of a normal one is near impossible if you are three inches tall, let alone a giant one covered in treasures. You won't get there and back in one night.' Her heart sank.

'She can!' Poco leapt up. 'I reckon with the right

equipment and a fierce heart, good company—'

'Shh Poco. It is impossible.' Opus shot him a stern look. 'Even for Numinkind.'

'What do you mean, Numinkind?' asked Nell.

'Numinkind are the secret guardians to humankind, of course.' He turned to her. 'Why, don't tell me, you don't know?' He moved towards her and peered at her closely. 'Goodness, did you just awaken today?' His eyes twinkled as he gazed into hers.

'Oh, I suppose I did. Last night. Yes!' She blinked at him. 'The fizzing and stuff?' She tingled again and wiggled her body. 'What does it mean?' Loud chattering spread through the singers, and excited whispers came from the branches around.

'First of all, welcome!' Opus threw his arms wide and beamed. 'Yes, I believe you are numin, Nell, like us. We are kindred spirits! This is good news! A new numin awakened! I feared we may be dying out! Well, we take many curious forms. Figures like you and I, desirable treasures, and mysterious objects.' He pointed at the kaleidoscope, then to the post box, which hung from the branch beneath them. It spat out another letter from its slot. 'We are as interesting and varied as the humans are. Isn't that wonderful? We work undercover in homes all around the world, to make human lives better.' He spread his arms out towards the town beyond. 'Awakening comes at a time of powerful human feelings. Joy or grief, or a wish from the one who loves us. Sound familiar?' Nell stared at him with wide eyes, her plan to make things right for Emma filling her thoughts.

'Yes! The tingling started when Emma made the wish! So, she brought me to life!' Nell spun around on the spot, stretching her arms out. The little singers' faces lit up. They clasped each other's hands and gazed at Nell with big eyes.

'That's it! Ha! But not only that. First, numins have been handmade with love. Second, you are given with love. Lastly, you are received with love and that seals the deal. Then, a wish from a human calls us for full numinhood. Boom!' He clapped. 'You are their full-time personal guardian! Ha! A little piece of Emma's soul has sparked up inside you, Nell! You have her qualities, with your own soul, your own heart!'

'So that's what I can feel!' Nell squashed her hands against her pounding chest. Her heart blazed like starlight. A bell swung above her in the breeze, tinkling against the multi-coloured baubles around. She caught sight of her reflection in it. 'Oh, I even look a little like Emma now!'

'We carry the fires of human life inside us!' Opus nodded and threw his staff in the air and caught it with the other hand. The others threw their instruments up and caught them, cheering, and clapping. Poco tried to do a backflip but ended up in a crumpled heap. Opus, looked wearily at him. Nell's eyes sparkled in the lights of the town and the tree as she admired the objects around them.

'I was a gift to Emma from her great-grandmother,' she said. She peered into the end of the kaleidoscope, tilting her head. The view inside was not of the beads and stones in its glass barrel, but of a meadow shimmering in the breeze. 'Wow,' she whispered.

'We are the love of many generations,' said Opus, his eyes shining. Nell looked down at her little body, and the brush marks of the forget-me-not flowers on her front.

'So, I am a numin!' she held her hand against her cheek.

'One of the team, ha!' said Opus, clapping his hands. Nell danced around with Poco and knocked into a glass dragonfly decoration with iridescent wings that glimmered in the lights. It woke and fluttered away between the glinting baubles. The sparkling violin drifted over them, playing a sweet song.

'That's a mood numin,' said Opus. 'The humans can't hear it, but the music alters their mood, bringing them joy or love, whatever they need. We are only ever for the good.' Delight danced inside her as the violin floated over. 'There are many kinds, as I am sure you will discover. I suspect you may be a heart numin, judging by your character.' He smiled warmly. Her face flushed pink.

'And you? When did you awaken?' asked Nell.

'Oh, us? We've been awake for hundreds of years!' He thrust out his chest and raised his chin. 'Still going strong!'

'Hundreds?' Nell's mouth dropped open.

'Ha ha, it goes by in a flash!'

As they talked, whispers spread through the branches above them at the new arrival to numinhood. A pair of pixies cackled and swung nearby on a clove orange hanging from red ribbons. The pixies were pale with pointed ears, webbed toes, knobbly knees, and glinting eyes. They were trying to swing it higher and higher, sending cloves flying. They waved to her with their spindly fingers. She waved back. A warm glow filled her as more numins came from the shadows and into view. The sloth listened with one eye open. A donkey chewed a frond of pine needles and spat the rest out below him. Two sausage dogs wearing red bandanas around their necks chased along the branch above. They poked their noses through the pine needles towards Nell and wagged their tails. She smiled and gave an awkward wave back to all of them. The strange figure she had met wasn't there. Relief trickled through her, and so did many more questions.

'I just need to make sure the angel heard the wish, then I'll go home. I know she will help us,' she said. One crow flapped by, this one with a toe missing. Its wings created a wind that sent the nearby baubles tinkling and bobbing into each other.

'Nell, I am afraid that this is not the whole story.' Opus' face shadowed with gloom. Nell tensed.

Just then, the streak of blue fire hurtled down and landed in between them. It exploded in a puff of pale blue sparks and smoke. When the air cleared, a small, scared-looking robin with golden dragon scales sat blinking up at them.

CHAPTER 5

ELF AND SAFETY

'Blinking Baubles!' said Nell. The robin hid behind a purple striped bauble and poked her head out. Shaking, its scales shimmered in the lights, its eyes glistening with tears. Nell rushed over and the others followed.

'Good grief,' said Opus.

'Are you alright?' asked Nell, squinting up to where she tumbled in. The robin held out her wing, which was bent, and whimpered. Nell knelt next to her and took it in her hands. 'Oh, no,' she said. The numins looked around into the shadows.

'It must be a fire numin! Hello, are you lost?' asked Opus rather close to her face. The robin coughed a cloud of grey smoke all over him. Opus spluttered and hurried behind Nell for safety.

'Back-fire numin more like,' chuckled Poco.

'There's something you don't see every day,' said Opus. 'How odd.' He peered up between the branches. 'What happened?' he asked from behind Nell. The trembling robin moved her good wing around as if telling a story in song. They nodded along politely.

'No idea what that's all about,' said Opus.

'Nope, not a clue!' said Poco, wiping his nose on his sleeve. Nell smoothed the robin's scaly wing in her hands.

'It's alright. I am Nell.' She held her hand to her chest. 'These are my friends,' she nodded to them. 'Let me help. This won't hurt,' she said. It was the sort of thing Emma's mother would say. She bent the wing quickly into its original position. The robin let out a shrill cry, then puffed out a billowing ball of white fire. 'Wooah!' said Nell, leaning out of the way as heat singed the pine needles nearby. The others watched from between their fingers. The robin stretched and wiggled her wing, then tumbled and swooped around Nell's head. She dropped beaky kisses and a rainbow of sparks onto her.

'Hey!' Nell laughed at the latest new sensation: tickling. The robin flew up through the branches, looping and waving until out of sight.

'Astonishing!' said Opus. 'She won't forget that you helped her, Nell. Fire numins have long memories.' He let out a long whistle. 'I must say, isn't it a pleasure to see all these numins, squad? It has been a long time!' He beamed at his group, who nodded and chattered, pointing all around them.

'Strange though, falling like that. Fire numin are intelligent, filled with passion and love. Their fiery heart sometimes leaves them rather, well, you saw! I wonder what happened.' He rested his finger on his chin. Nell gazed up into the darkness after the robin, an uneasiness tightening her tummy. She curled her plait through her fingers as the baubles above tinkled in the breeze the robin left behind.

'I bet the angel is a fire numin too,' she said, her eyes full of hope. 'You were saying something, Opus, about the angel?'

'Ah, yes. Angels are mysterious creatures. Fickle.' He placed his tiny hand on her arm. 'The thing is, we don't know if she is alive, or numin or whatever. I am afraid it's likely she is only decorative, like most things on this tree.' He flicked his gold staff at a silver holly leaf, which spun in circles.

'Of course she's real. Emma wouldn't make a wish on a random thing,' said Nell. 'She's a clever girl.' She studied a bauble with a nativity scene painted on it. It had a glittering angel hovering in the sky painted above the stable. She traced her finger over it. 'See, an angel.' Opus leaned in, admiring the detail. 'And didn't the mayor say she's real?'

'Well, I'm not sure she said that, exactly,' said Opus, with a worried expression. 'There was one once, you know, a Numin angel. But that was centuries ago.' He looked out over the town and tapped his chin.

'Well, there you are then.' Nell straightened up, courage sparking inside. 'Thank you for filling me in. I must go now.' She looked at her wrist as if she was wearing a watch. 'One freckle past the hair, ha ha!' She tried to hide a yawn behind her hand, then tested the strength of a gold cord hanging from above.

'Nell,' said Opus, 'awakening is exhausting. Rest before you go. Numins need sleep too, you know! We take on many human traits. It can be annoying; sneezing, burping and so forth, but you have to take the rough with the smooth. Wait until morning. It is a treacherous journey. You will need all your strength.' He looked up, then out towards the crows along the railings, flapping their wings, and fighting occasionally. 'And it's odd for them to flock like this.' He looked back to Nell. 'We will accompany you as far as that overhanging branch first thing tomorrow.' He pointed to a large branch higher up around the tree. 'It will be too tricky for us after that, and we might hold you up. We are so glossy, you see. We might slip.' He stroked his coat with a proud smile. 'And just look at our puny arms, ha!' Whoever made us did not have tree-climbing in mind!' Nell smiled.

'Oh, here we go!' said Poco, rolling his eyes. 'Puny arms now? I would come all the way Nell, but Opus is obsessed with health and safety. Or elf and safety, as I like to call it. Ha ha!'

'Poco, you know we would only slip through the branches.' Opus glared at him. 'That time you went into space with that astronaut was one of the worst days in our lives,' said Opus. 'Tim something-or-other.'

'My space trip was an accident!' Poco frowned, his hands firmly on his hips.

'You jumped into his pocket!' He closed his eyes

and pinched the bridge of his nose. Nell laughed behind her hand.

'I fell in! I was trying to get closer to listen at that Hawthorn House Christmas party. He knocked into the tree, and I fell! It wasn't my fault he took me into space as his lucky charm!' Nell gaped at him.

'You've been to space?' Her eyes were on stalks.

'The view was fantastic! Getting to the top of this tree will be a breeze,' he said, rocking back on his heels. 'You'll nail it.' She looked up at the stars and whistled.

'He had a taste of the high life, you see Nell, and it has brought nothing but trouble.' Opus turned to Poco. 'You are not going,' he said through gritted teeth as Poco huffed. He faced Nell and softened his voice.

'Rest. Keep that flame of your soul burning bright. Plenty of time.' He smiled.

'Alright,' said Nell, realising her limbs ached like lead weights. She yawned as she climbed inside a small felt stocking, tucking it up to her chin. The musicians huddled together on the branch under the velvety sky, with the cold air curling around them. Opus placed his staff in the middle, which crackled like a campfire. He poked at it with a pine needle as if it were real. Their faces glowed in its light. The sausage dog decorations snuggled up on a ribbon-tied cinnamon stick hanging behind, the sloth snoring above. The pixies were sticking their fingers in each other's ears, stopping each other from sleeping. Nell laughed and relaxed into the stocking, burying her face in its fluffy top. The soft felt warmed her cheek, though not as much as the blanket of friendship her new friends had given her.

'I am so happy to have found you.' She smiled and closed her eyes.

'Us too dear Nell. We are going to be great friends!' The numins fell asleep under the glow of Opus's staff. One numin, though, watched and listened from the dark shadows above them.

CHAPTER 6

POOR OLD RED

After a night of scattered dreams, Nell woke to the sound of loud and rather disgusting throat-clearing. The choir had settled themselves into a semi-circle towards the edge of the branch and sang the song Oh, Christmas Tree. Opus used his staff to keep time. Their beautiful harmonies floated through the crisp winter air. It reminded her of the music Emma's mother played on the nights that she couldn't sleep. She stretched the night from her arms and legs as the music drifted through her.

The winter sun speckled light across the tree, melting frost into beads of dew. The watery spheres reflected a thousand tiny Christmas trees inside them. Colours and lights winked at them from all sides.

Some of the numin folk gathered on the branches nearby to listen. A group of turtledove ornaments swooped and danced around a mirror ball. Nell waved, and they waved their wings back to her. The pixies wobbled on a loop of tinsel, singing along with their own rude alternative words, sniggering. The sloth tapped her foot as she snored. A heart made from ruby-red dried cranberries twirled in the breeze and shone like jewels in the rising sun. The sausage dogs weaved in and out of it, playing tag.

The singers finished their song to loud applause.

'That was beautiful!' she said as she clapped. The choir flushed various shades of pink.

'Thank you. Just a few centuries of practice, ha! Are we ready?'

'Yep!' said Nell, flapping her arms by her sides. The singers smiled and jostled together into a line. The pixies came closer, picking their noses and showing the contents to each other.

'Right,' said Opus, turning his back to the pixies. He lowered his voice. 'Just ignore them. I don't even think they are numins.' He pulled down a piece of red and white string. He wrapped it around each of the choir's wooden bodies, so they were held together in a line. They chattered excitedly, apart from Poco.

'For goodness' sake,' he said, 'always bothering and fussing.' Nell tried not to laugh.

'Eight numin musicians at the ready?' bellowed Opus, ignoring Poco too. They threw their instruments in the air and caught them again.

'Check!'

'One safety line!' He tugged at the rope.

'Check!' The choir tugged it too, joking and pulling each other about.

'One newly awakened and fantastically brave numin!'

'Check!' said Nell, her arm in the air and her chin high, a big grin on her face.

'A journey of a thousand miles begins with a single step!' Opus held up his star staff and winked at Nell. The staff fizzed and a flare of white light flashed out from it. Nell laughed. They ducked under a golden pear and trotted across the branches with Nell and Opus at the front. Poco was at the back, untying himself from the group.

They picked their way along the middle of the stems to avoid being spiked. The branches grew in rows and layers in some places and swooped down like mountainsides in others. Opus used his staff as a hook to move the branches down to hop on. They helped each other, moving steadily upwards across the front of the tree with Riverside Square to one side.

'Keep out of sight of the humans, a little away from the edges. If they see us moving, well, you know what humans are like! They would catch us, put us under fancy domes, dress us in silly clothes, sell us, you name it! A human sighting takes a lot of undoing work, I can tell you!'

'Emma would never do that,' said Nell.

As they walked, some of the choir whispered to each other while pointing out to the crows. Nell leaned closer to listen. She could just about make out the words 'snatcher' and 'Red.'

'What's a snatcher?' she asked. 'And what is Red?' Opus's face grew crimson. He shot them a glare and avoided Nell's gaze. An uneasy feeling coiled in her tummy.

'Come on, it's rude to whisper.' Opus stopped and sighed.

'Very well, Nell. We never told you what happened to our old friend, poor old Red.' His mouth hardened to a thin line. The other musicians clutched each other's hands and shoulders and shifted about.

'I didn't want to scare you last night, but you should know. He wasn't as lucky as you.' He took a deep breath. 'Red was a numin elf, one of the Christmas squad back at Hawthorn House. Always friendly, funny too. Wore red all over, of course. Named by an unimaginative human as you can tell.' He beckoned her closer. Nell leant in and turned her ear to him. 'Snatchers don't care if you're kind or funny, do they?' Opus closed his eyes.

'Snatchers?' Nerves inched across her chest.

'Red had belonged to a boy who moved abroad. Left behind in the rush to leave, you see. He was a practical numin, full of great ideas. Lucky for us, he ended up in the Christmas decorations trunk back at Hawthorn House. He lived there with us, until–' He held his hand up to his forehead, his eyes glistening. 'Don't think that the good always have happy lives, Nell.' Poco pushed in front of Opus and spoke in a trembling voice.

'One day, a sweaty hand reached into our Christmas tree and plucked him right out!' He showed the action, jerking his arm back with a terrible grimace. Nell gulped. One of the singers, Melody, stepped in, her voice high.

'That weasel of a boy chucked him about, then threw him into the gutter outside. Like a piece of rubbish!'

Melody mimicked throwing something down, then held her teary face in her hands.

'Ooh!' The choir joined in clutching their heads, wet with tears. 'Poor Red!' they cried.

'Poor Red. I am sorry.' She placed her hand on Melody's shoulder and patted her.

'And then, from nowhere,' said Opus, 'a crow flew in and swept him up! Right in his beak! Like what happened to you, Nell! But he carried poor Red off with his legs dangling and flailing about.' He swallowed. 'We never saw him again.' The choir sobbed into each other's armpits and comforted each other.

'Every year we look out for him when they take us out of hibernation for the Christmas celebrations. We still hope he will return, but it's been so long–' Opus closed his eyes. Poco put his arm around him.

'That is so sad.' She patted him and promised herself she would be careful. She couldn't afford to get snatched. Emma had too much to lose. Opus nodded. 'I do hope you find him again.'

'Being separated from your human means death for most of us, after a while. Back to an ordinary state. But he thrived with us.' He looked out at the crows. 'You were lucky. This tree is full of wonderful fellows, but not all. You get numin snatchers too. There to help themselves, and their less pleasant human owners. Be warned, Nell.' He checked around them and lowered his voice to a whisper. 'There may well be snatchers both on and off the tree.'

'And evil creatures–' Poco jumped up and spoke, 'with sharp teeth and eyes that look like they want to pull the wings of small, helpless things.' He wrung his hands and looked over each of his shoulders. 'Numins gone bad!' He rounded and raised his arms to look more menacing. Nell's mouth was now dry.

'Creatures that eat their victims, for fun.' Melody quivered, pointing out towards the crows, and then into the depths of the tree.

'Alright, alright.' Opus nodded, holding his hand out to shush them as they huddled together.

'I already saw a numin I didn't like the look of,' said Nell. 'When I arrived. That's why I came back to you.'
'Quite right too. Trust your gut, Nell! Don't get too close, you understand?' She nodded. 'Numin magic is ancient and beautiful. But without love, it can become twisted. And the crows already have their eyes on you,' he said. 'Who knows what else?'

CHAPTER 7

WHY THE MONA LISA SMILED

They heard occasional rustling from inside the tree. Nearer the outside, the crows watched in the distance. Poco showed Nell how to do cartwheels along the centre of the branches. Nell showed him Emma's robotic dancing that she always wanted to try. Neither was very good, but it didn't matter. The warmth of new friendship swirled around them like sunshine.

They passed a shimmering peacock decoration in rich turquoise and purple sequins. It stared vacantly forward as it turned eerily in the air, like a ghost. Nell shivered. An African guinea fowl carving pecked at a chocolate coin with a puzzled expression, making it spin. A silk Indian elephant with a colourful embroidered saddle and a green tassel hanging on his forehead stood on one leg, his eyes closed, his arms in the air. Nell nodded politely to him and wondered if Emma's mother might ever be able to go to her yoga class again. Opus turned to her.

'Hope's Ends' humans brought their most treasured possessions here, which tend to be numins. They feel so desperate. It is rather exciting.' He quivered at the thought and turned to Nell. 'Some bring protection, some luck, healing, love, or hope. Dream whispering ideas and comfort in tough times, even before we awake.' Nell remembered whispering soothing words and ideas to Emma in the night, so she would wake up feeling stronger. 'We take their worries away on the wind. Sometimes we defend against bad energy. Once we awaken, we complete missions, perform magic, invisibility, time travel.'

'Time travel?' Nell whistled. She ran her fingers over some old silver tinsel that twinkled in the winter sunlight and danced in the breeze. 'Amazing the humans haven't noticed you after all this time!'

'I know! They are so caught up with what they call real life, as they call it, Nell, ha! If only they knew!'

They hopped up to the next branch. A family of little grey mice decorations wearing scarves and jumpers bounced past them, giggling, and rolling about, carrying skis and poles. One mouse hopped over a loop of red ribbon that was looped along a nearby branch. Nell took hold of the end and swung it in circles like a skipping rope. The laughing mouse jumped over it a few times, then scurried on through the needles after the others.

'Numins can do anything,' said Poco. 'Some of my friends got quite famous!' Melody clapped her hands together.

'Oh, oh!' she said. 'Remember that artist's numin in Florence, who stood on his shoulder to make the Mona Lisa smile during her portrait? That painting was going to be awful without that!'

'There are often disasters if we aren't around,' said Poco. 'Like the time that numin popped out for a few minutes from his home in Pudding Lane?' Nell's eyes lit with anticipation. Melody put her head in her hands. Opus glared at them.

'Let's just tell encouraging stories, shall we?'

'Like the numin of the captain of the Titanic?' asked Melody. Opus shot her a hard look.

'Not that one!'

'What about Sir Isaac Newton's apple?' said Poco.

'Alright, yes,' he said, relief washing over his face.

'Newton was a scientist. He had been ripe for a great idea all year. His numin saw him sit down under an apple tree that day. The numin called in a few numin friends, including me, to help. I had to sneak out, of course.' Poco looked at Opus who avoided his gaze. 'We bounced up and down on the branch until an apple fell on Sir Isaac's head.' He jumped about, causing Nell to wobble. She laughed and grabbed hold of the pine needles to steady herself.

'He discovered gravity! Thanks to numins!' laughed Nell.

'Indeed,' said Opus through a broad smile.

They walked along in silence, hopping upwards from one branch to the next until a wide gap appeared in front of them, with the overhanging branch on the other side. They lined up along the edge. Nell's tummy flipped, as they all tried not to look down into the narrow gorge that stretched below them. Poco stared down and let out a long whistle. A trumpet dangled in the gap ahead, tied to a long red cord from above. It turned expectantly. Nell swallowed. She took a steadying breath to calm the nerves quivering inside.

The branch ahead curved downwards like a headland. A collection of baubles hung above. A pearly glass moon, complete with craters. A velvet bauble the colour of sapphire, with crystal stars arranged in the shape of the constellations. A green and blue sphere, the earth, with a shimmering turquoise sea which rippled. Waves and bubbling white surf rose and dipped between its tiny green countries. Another in the shape of Saturn twisted gently next to it, surrounded by eight hovering rings.

Underneath the collection a reindeer decoration with one antler stood on the tip of the branch. He had brown fuzzy fur that was worn in places, with bald patches and a scar where his missing antler had once been. He watched the crows on the railings, and the green clouds now floating beyond the river. Just above perched a model of a pure white feathered dove, with silver wing tips and shining onyx eyes. Nell's eyes moved to the reindeer, who turned to face the new arrivals. He bowed to Nell, his eyes twinkling. Butterflies swirled in her core, and she bowed back.

CHAPTER 8

THE OLD FELLOWSHIP

'Ahoy friends!' called the reindeer, his eyes glinting like drops of melted chocolate.

'Ahoy!' called Opus.

'Hello!' said Nell, waving shyly.

'I'm Indy,' said the reindeer. His voice gave her the feeling of sliding into a pool of still water.

'My name's Nell.' The dove fluttered down and landed on the reindeers' remaining antler, bowing to them over her snow-white wing, making a tinkling sound as she moved.

'And I am Ava,' she said.

'And we are the Hawthorn House Miniature Choir.' They each gave a low bow.

'It's good to meet you at last,' said Ava. 'You are one of the oldest treasures in the area.' Ava's voice sounded like an oboe. The singers looked proudly from one to the other.

'That's right,' said Opus.

'We have a book about the curiosities of Hawthorn House in the bookshop. At least, we did before it closed down,' she said, fluffing up her feathers.

'Bobs Books?' said Nell.

'Yes, that's it.'

'That is where Emma's mother worked.' She nudged Poco. Ava smiled at Nell.

'I am the bell above the door,' she said, and wriggled so she rang. 'Emma's mother must be Sara.'

'Yes, that's her!'

'I can't bear to see Bob without his shop.' Ava fluffed her feathers again and looked out to the town.

'We are delivering our brave friend Nell, who is off to see the angel,' said Opus. Indy poked a branchlet above with his antler so that the rope with the trumpet swung towards Nell.

'The angel? She is alive?' His eyes sparkled.

'I think so, I mean, yes. Emma wished on her. I am going to make sure it comes true.' She tried to ignore the doubt that curled inside. 'Or they will have to leave town.'

'I see. My owners' nephews can't visit for fear they might get ill,' said Indy. 'Those boys keep me going, these days. My owner grew up a long time ago and doesn't need me now. He travelled with me all over the world, though these days is mostly works in an office.' He looked down. 'If my nephews aren't allowed to visit, I'm not sure what will happen to me.' He coughed.

'Oh dear,' said Nell, twisting her hair.

'And no-one visits Hawthorn House anymore.' Opus shook his head. 'Our sweet caretaker is so sad. They may have to sell the house you know, and all its contents, after centuries! What will happen to us, to him?' They all shivered, and fell into a thoughtful silence.

'Maybe the angel will help all of us,' said Nell.

'Are you going to the fellowship meeting?' asked Ava. Opus's eyes lit up.

'What fellowship meeting?' he asked. He and the choir shuffled excitedly.

'We hear that Vaspar, the fourth king, is holding a meeting about starting a numin fellowship, up over there somewhere.' She waved with her wing. 'We don't know him, but we are going to go.'

Nell knelt by the edge and studied the trumpet swing. Poco crouched by her side, both working out how best to make use of it.

'The fourth king, you say?' asked Opus.

'He was a spare.' Ava shrugged.

'Oh dear, ha! Well, this is the first numin gathering in centuries. Wouldn't it be wonderful if the old numin fellowship reformed? Just in time for this crisis!' He turned to Nell. 'Numins used to help each other through hard times, and good. We had a thriving numin society!'

'I am too young,' said Indy, 'but Ava told me all

about the great community it once was.'

'We have a once in a lifetime chance gathered here on this tree,' said Opus. 'To get the great fellowship going again. If we did, I'll bet we could sort out this mess in no time,' he arced his arm out towards the town. 'We have stopped wars, you know!' Indy and Ava nodded, while the musicians chattered.

'If we could put our heads together, solutions will come,' said Indy.

'That would be a relief,' said Nell. 'I will ask the angel for help for the town too.' Nell blushed as they all smiled at her. 'What happened to the old fellowship?' she asked.

'Over the last hundred years or so, there are fewer treasures being handmade. That means fewer numins, and fewer links between households. Factories make things cheaper, and, well, not bad, let's face it,' he prodded a model of a Christmas tree covered in sparkling jewels. 'Beautiful, but lifeless. And everything the same!' He pointed a few branches higher to an identical one. 'That is all very handy, but the fellowship shrank to nothing. Sometimes, you don't know what you've got until it's gone.' He looked at his feet and then to Nell.

'Oh, Nell,' said Opus, turning to her and squeezing her arms. 'The things numins can do!' He gazed out into the square with his hand on his chest. 'And now, the fellowship may be this town's hope of an answer.' He looked back at Ava and Indy. 'You'll have to fill us in after the meeting. We can't get up that far!' He reached out his staff and pulled the trumpet swing towards them. Nell took it in her shaking hand.

'Looks like after all this time, Hope's End hasn't lost its numins at all! And here we are, together!' He held his arms out to Indy and Ava on the other side of the gap, who smiled back. The choir looked at each other and held each other's hands. Nell's heart lit with hope.

*

Poco and Melody grinned as they held the trumpet for Nell to climb on. She took a deep breath.

'I think it will hold you!' said Poco, his eyes gleamed.

'You think it will hold me?' Nell looked down, trying to ignore the riot of nerves now flaming inside. 'Oh, I shouldn't have looked!' She squeezed her eyes shut.

'Some numins used it earlier. It is safe,' said Ava, smiling.

'Take this,' Opus tucked his staff into the back of her jumper. He winked. 'In case it comes in handy. It is an excellent light in dark places. Just point, it'll know what to do.' Nell hugged him tight.

'Thank you, Opus!' She gazed at its shimmering golden surface; it looked as if it was made from thousands of tiny stars. She hugged Poco and Melody and waved to the others. She hopped onto the trumpet and leant back.

'I'll push,' said Poco, hopping about on the spot.

'Geronimo!' She pushed off with a boost from Poco. The cool air whooshed past her ears, her legs sticking out in front of her, her plaits swishing behind. 'Woohoo!' she cried. She leapt off, landing on the soft branches next to Indy and Ava, who steadied her. She lay for a moment, looking up at Saturn, the moon, and the earth above, catching her breath. Applause filled the air, Poco clapping the longest. Opus placed his hand on his heart.

'We believe in you Nell!'

Just then, the robin flapped in, showering a rainbow of sparks over Nell. She wrapped her scaly wings around her in a tight hug, before landing on the moon bauble near Ava.

'Oh, ha ha! Hello!' said Nell.

'This is Ruby, she belongs to the woman from the boat.' Ava nodded out towards one of the boats that rocked gently on the silvery river, the scent of baking bread floating out of it. Ruby sang to Ava and flapped her wings about. Ava nodded.

'She says thank you. Earlier some beetles attacked her, though we aren't sure why. You helped her.'

'I'm glad you're alright,' said Nell. Ruby exploded a shower of rainbow sparks around her. Nell giggled. The little singers put their hands on their hearts and walked away, waving behind them. 'And take care of that lovely new soul of yours! Ha!'

'Bon voyage!' said Poco. Nell waved as her friends wandered away. She smiled up at Indy, who looked impressed. She blushed.

'You are brave, Nell,' said Indy. 'I'll be keeping watch around here if you need anything.'

'Thank you,' she said, 'goodbye.' He lifted his front hoof politely, then turned to watch the crows again.

'Good luck Nell,' said Ava. She bowed again and flapped her wings, making Indy's fur ripple. She flew off with Ruby looping behind her, sparking trails of gold.

Nell climbed upwards through the dark needles until the others were out of sight. The sound of the song Little Donkey drifted after her until the quiet of the tree closed around her.

CHAPTER 9

THE CURIOUS TREASURES IN THE BRANCHES

Nell moved from branch to branch in an upward spiral around the tree. Nearer the trunk, the needles thickened and spiked so densely she could not pass through with ease. She used Opus's staff to pull herself up, and whatever she could find. On a higher branch, a long line of sheep ornaments with fluffy white wool coats hurried along. Nell ducked underneath a gold pouch which had deep blue spirals embroidered all over it.

'Oh,' she said. She tried to open it. It growled and bit her as if it were a wild animal. 'Ow!' She pulled her fingers away. 'Savage! I was only looking!' she said as she rubbed her hand.

Near the pouch hung a snow globe. Inside was a

herd of tiny sandy unicorns grazing on the tundra. 'There really are many kinds of numin, aren't there?'

She balanced along a fairy lights string with her arms stretched out to the sides. She was now climbing up the side of the tree that faced the river. She knocked into the next branch, sending a dented tin Santa flying. 'Oops!'

'Oi! Get your own branch!' he said when he finished spluttering. He was red and round with pink chubby cheeks and a thick cloudy beard. He tried to clamber back on to the branch and muttered under his breath, 'I don't have time for you, fool.'

'I am sorry, sir!' said Nell, wondering what he normally did with his time. She tried to give him a leg-up, hooking him up again. She made it worse, tangling his leg in the hook so that he hung upside down.

'Argh! Nincompoop!' he said, then he muttered rude words to himself.

"Oh, dear, I–' she said. 'I was only trying to help.'

'Well, don't,' he spat. The Santa untangled himself and spun himself back into position. He scratched himself on the behind and turned his back to her.

'Sorry!' said Nell. 'I wonder if that's the real Father Christmas?' she chuckled to herself, leaving him red-faced and shaking his fist at her.

She came to a wide, flat branch with a pretty wreath of holly and rosemary hanging at one end. A glittering sprout hurtled through the air and landed on Nell's head.

'Ow!' She rubbed her head and frowned.

'Out of the way!' said the sprout, nodding towards

the wreath. 'I was about to go in goal!' A group of numins sprinted over. A nutcracker in the shape of a soldier in front. He had black eyebrows and bright eyes, with tufts of hair on either side of his head, a red coat and matching hat. Next to him was a polar bear so slim that it must have been a bookmark. Behind them was a hare with a pretty moustache and wire glasses. He sprinted with the model of a red post box spitting its tiny letters out that she had seen earlier. The nutcracker, whose jaw dangled from his face in a way that made Nell wince, said:

'On me head!' The post box kicked the sprout over to him, letting out another splutter of letters with his words written on them.

'Wheeee!' screeched the sprout as she whizzed through the air. The polar bear tackled the nutcracker, who kicked the grinning sprout through the leafy wreath. Nell covered her eyes.

'Goal!' The nutcracker slid on his knees across the branch and punched the air. 'Ever played sproutball?' he laughed. Nell laughed too.

'Come on, join in!' said the sprout. 'Don't worry about me, I love it!' They played together for a while and Nell scored three goals. She talked to them about the fellowship and her trip to the angel. The nutcracker's name was Otto, and the Post-box was Mick. The sprout was just Sprout. The hare was Kevin, and the bookmark was Anka. She waved goodbye to her new friends and set off again, limbs buzzing, across the quiet branches.

'Good luck!' they called after her.

As she travelled, noises seemed to follow her

from the shadows inside the tree. Nell's mind wandered to the mysterious arrow that flew out when the crow took her, and to poor Red, the crows and possible snatchers. Her skin crawled. She pushed a flickering lotus flower ornament out of the way and looked up. Above, branches stretched up to what seemed like forever, as if the top was moving further and further away. She still couldn't see the angel, and she balled her hands in frustration.

Eventually, she passed to the part of the tree where the sun never shone. The sound of low, dull tinkling filled the air, as glass icicles knocked against each other. Her neck prickled. The scent of cool peppermint soaked her senses and made her dizzy. She sneezed, felt as if she was floating for a moment, then drifted asleep where she stood.

CHAPTER 10

GLACIA AND THE SUGAR MICE

Nell woke feeling groggy, as if after an uneasy dream. Frost had painted the tree silver, which twinkled against the lights. She sleepily wandered across the shimmering branches into a glade thick with glass icicles and snowflake decorations. The icicles were sharp and created a harsh light. A cold tickle moved down Nell's back as she pushed her way through the glinting ice-cold spears. Shivering, she was about to change direction when a ballerina appeared ahead, spinning on her toes.

Nell stared, butterflies flitting in her tummy, as the dancer twirled in perfect circles. She wore the palest blue satin and a white tulle tutu with a delicate snowflake pattern. Ice crystals hovered and glistened around her. Her silver hair was swept into a tight bun, with more glittering crystals wrapped around it. She had timeless beauty, the type who might be chosen by a Tudor king. The kind of king who beheaded people. Made of china, she had a mouth no bigger than a tiny pink dot. Around her feet scurried three tiny white sugar-mice, running in circles. Nell let out another enormous sneeze. She realised she was not dreaming. She shook her head from side to side to wake herself up. The ballerina stopped turning.

'What have we here? A sweet little creature!' she said. Her voice sounded like an untuned harp. Nell's mouth had dropped open, staring with her arms dangling by her side, bewitched by her beauty. She pulled herself together and spoke.

'Hello, I'm Nell. I am on my way to see the angel.' She looked down at her feet, though she wasn't sure why.

'I'm Glacia. Good afternoon,' said the ballerina, extending her arm into an elegant arc over her head. She wound her legs together as she danced en pointe, giggling for no reason. When she smiled, the corners of her mouth turned down. 'Pleased to meet you.' She reached out her arm to shake hands, then as she studied Nell more closely, frowned and pulled her arm away. She peered at the blue flowers painted on Nell's jumper. 'Little weeds, are they?'

'They are forget-me-nots.' Nell's cheeks burned at the insult, and to discover that it was already the afternoon. Glacia stepped back, giving a breezy laugh.

'Sweet!' she said. 'Visiting the angel, you say?'

'Yes.' Nell pointed upwards with a goofy smile. 'I have something to ask her.'

'Speak up!'

'I want to ask for the angels' help.'

'You, speak to an angel! Delightful!' She clasped her hands together, looking Nell up and down again. Her icy eyes tried to meet Nell's, who looked away, a thousand uncomfortable knots tied inside her.

'What will you ask her? Don't worry.' She brushed her hand along the edge of Nell's face. 'You can tell me.' Nell squirmed and pulled away. Glacia scrunched up her nose and laughed. Nell took a calming breath.

'Well, Emma, my owner made a wish to the angel. To stay in their home and not leave before Christmas. It's a long story. I want to make sure it comes true.'

'Oh dear, that is so sweet, and such a shame.'

'It is?' Nell stiffened.

'There is no such thing as a wish, child. Or an angel, not really. There used to be rumours about a numin angel long ago, but that was all talk.' She scrunched up her nose and smiled. 'Shame! Poor you on a wasted journey!' She might as well have thrown cold water over her. 'And poor Emma. You left her! You know, you won't ever see her again. Sounds as if you've broken the bond.' Nell's heart sank like a lead weight.

'What?' She gulped. 'That's not possible. I–'

'Once you decide to leave your human, the bond

breaks. You no longer part of them. Oh, dear. Didn't you know? You're on your own now.'

'No,' croaked Nell. Her mouth had gone dry. 'That's not true.' She remembered something Opus said about separation from your human. 'But I didn't leave her. I am going back to her once I have finished.' She trembled. Glacia admired an icicle hanging nearby. She held a finger beneath its sharp tip and moved it around, reflecting shards of light that hurt Nell's eyes.

'It probably isn't your fault. Sometimes they want us gone.' She lifted her hand and studied her fingernails. The colour drained from Nell's face. 'She willed you to leave on an impossible journey. Getting older, was she? Children are so stupid, aren't they?' She sneered, and admired her nails on her other hand. Nell blinked at her, aghast.

'Yes, but she wouldn't want to–' Glacia stroked Nell's head. 'That's it isn't it. They grow up. There comes a time in most numins lives where they are no longer needed. The owner will unknowingly wish us away from them. Or throw us out and forget about us.' Her voice was crisp. 'There are many lost numin. Drifters with no real home. It isn't only you.' She smiled.

'It isn't me at all!' blasted Nell, now crimson. 'I only awakened yesterday and–' she held back tears. 'It can't be, I–'

'Yesterday?' Glacia shot her a look. A wry smile crossed her face. 'So, you are new.' She tapped her finger against her lip. 'Interesting. Anyway, of course they don't need us forever. Don't worry. Lost numin can find another way to live. Alone in the shadows and in the underground. For a while, at least. Until they–' she sighed and looked up at the sky. 'I mean, the bond may remain sometimes. But only in very exceptional cases.' She eyed Nell up and down. 'That really is only in exceptional cases.' She pulled her mouth into a sad face. 'Too sad,' she said.

Nell sank down onto the branch. She looked at her flaking forget-me-nots design, and the smudges on her body. She realised how old fashioned and tatty she was compared to Glacia. Perhaps she was wished away, and headed for doom. For death. And she had hardly even got started with life.

'If you do go on your silly journey, you would find a pretty piece of tin up there. That so-called angel was a bad choice for the tree. Clunky.' She narrowed her eyes as she looked towards the top. 'Our silly mayor always had poor taste and embarrassing ideas.' Her voice became harder. 'The humans don't understand anything. I am afraid this town will fall further into ruin. I mean, a giant Christmas tree can hardly change a town's fortune, can it! Pah!' She spun on her points again with her arms arced rigidly above her. 'And there was a mix up as I have ended up here near the back where no one can see me! Ridiculous! And we all have to hang around out here in the wind and rain, with snatchers and what have you.' She rolled her eyes. 'Anyway.' She turned to Nell. 'The branches at the top of these trees will be almost impossible for numin. I know, I was once–' a pained expression flashed across her face.

Nell thought of Opus, Poco and Indy and Ava's

encouragement. Emma's smiling face flashed through her mind, and her wish. Her heart lifted.

'Well, I may as well give it a try!' Glacia checked something invisible on her elbow, and turned to give her a cold stare.

'Since you are new, I will help you. Visit Vaspar.' She pointed up to the opposite side of the tree. 'He is wonderful! Modelled on one of the wise men. He's founding the fellowship again.' Glacia picked a piece of dust from Nell's shoulder.

'I heard about the meeting,' said Nell. 'Though I have my own important meeting.' She pointed upwards and blushed. Glacia tapped her already neat hair into place.

'Thank you, Glacia. You have been most— helpful.' She bowed, then pushed past and onward through the icicles. 'Bye, have a nice day,' she said over her shoulder.

'Goodbye. Good luck!' she said icily. As Nell moved off, Glacia spun on her toes with her elegant arms stretched overhead, the sugar mice circling her. 'Watch out for snatchers!' she crowed with a cold smile. Each time she turned, she fixed her eyes on Nell, until she was out of sight.

'Typical! How can I have awakened and lost Emma already?' She held her palms out. 'I have broken my bond and I'm going to die! How can I be so stupid?' She flapped her hands by her sides. 'I wish I was more, you know, together. Like her.' She pointed back in Glacia's direction. 'Neater, with a talent! That dancing, wow!' She clasped her hands together. 'And those clothes! Gosh, she was beautiful. Perhaps I will see if I can tidy myself up a bit after all this.' She smoothed down her hair and her jumper. 'I bet she doesn't talk to herself either! But I know she's wrong. The angel is alive. I can feel it.' She clutched her heart. 'I will prove it, Emma!' She gave a firm nod and continued up, though it was difficult to ignore the uncertainty still twisting deep inside.

CHAPTER 11

POCO AND THE RED BARON

Nell moved back into the light. The blue-green branches brushed against each other, lapping like waves against the shore. A dolphin decoration with a blue shimmering body jumped over her and back into the branches as if into the waves and spray. She pulled back the branch to look for the angel. Instead, there hung a little wooden house model with a red roof and green trees outside. A home. Longing pulled at her heart. Perhaps Emma was glad she had gone and was getting on with her life. The sound of a woodpecker drilled through the air.

For some time, there was rustling in the shadows. She looked behind, and checked the inside of the tree towards the trunk.

'Nothing there,' she whispered. She passed underneath an hourglass, whose sand inside shifted upwards, even when she turned it over.

As she climbed a spiky branch, the rustling grew loud. She looked behind her where a little car with Red Baron written along the side zig-zagged along the branch. It spluttered and banged as it speeded towards her. Inside, the pixies, who now wore tiny sunglasses they found somewhere, cackled. They sped up and drove straight into Nell, knocking her flying onto the branch below.

'Oops. Sorry!' They sniggered. 'Not! Heh heh!'

'Hey!' Winded, Nell landed flat on her back. The pixies gawped down at her from the branch above, their large eyes glinting, grins spread over their faces. Her churning tummy caught up with her as the pixies gave each other a high five.

'You two are menaces!' she said, heat flushing her face. She stood up and shook out her legs and arms, hoping it would stop her head from spinning. The pixies shrugged, and let down a piece of tinsel for her to climb, which she did. She grumbled words Emma wasn't allowed to say as the pixies pulled up the tinsel with Nell hanging on.

'Oh, you are soooo heavy!' said one. They both grunted as they heaved, puffing, and panting unnecessarily.

'Oi!' said Nell, red in the face and fuming. 'Don't be rude!' They fell to their knees, wheezing with laughter. She reached the branch and clambered on; her eyebrows drawn into a scowl. It was all such a commotion that she didn't notice Poco sitting tucked in the back of the car. He had wrapped himself in a red tartan cloth. He was blushing and trying to hide. Nell put her hands on her hips.

'Poco! I thought you knew better!'

'Sorry, Nell, I didn't know they were going to be such reckless drivers.' He got out of the car and slammed the door. A wheel fell off. 'Truly terrible.' He rubbed the back of his neck. 'Fun though!' He grinned.

'I thought you were too small and slippery for journeys on trees?'

'Glossy, yes.' He looked down at himself. 'Not too glossy, though. I wanted to find you. I'm good at this stuff. And I want to visit the angel too.' A serious expression crossed his face. 'Opus always worries, but I have never seen him like this. He keeps muttering about the crisis. He thinks Hawthorn House will be sold and keeps saying "*what will become of us?*" He says the town's only hope is a numin fellowship to help the humans, and us, avoid certain doom. And he has been going on and on about the great angel of olden times since you left, saying "*if only.*" I can't bear it! So, as the bravest of the Hawthorn House crew, I am coming.' He folded his arms. 'To get the angel on our side. To make sure we get the fellowship back. It is Opus who is frightened about falling through the branches, of death. Not me. I love it. Not death, but I don't mind falling. I've only ever fallen off a tree 87 times and I'm fine!' He crossed his arms. Nell's heart softened.

'I am not sure that the pixies are the best choice of company,' she said, raising an eyebrow. They were now having a breath holding competition, turning from white to purple to blue.

'I am coming.' Poco stamped his foot. One of the pixies was now using the wheel to bash the other's head with. 'And we can give you a lift.' He nodded towards the car.

'I am not getting in that!' said Nell, her eyes almost bulging out of her head.

'Why? It's fine! Just a few scratches.' He kicked it. There was a large explosion and a puff of black, stinking smoke shot out of the back of the car. 'Oh.' He shifted from foot to foot, then clasped his hands together and crouched in front of her. 'Please can I come with you?' He held his face up to Nell and blinked at her with his bright, shining eyes, as sweetly as he could. 'Together?' Nell looked at him, then rolled her eyes.

'Alright,' she said. Poco punched the air. Three geese flapped passed them, with green gingham bows around their necks. They were followed by a little hedgehog pin cushion with pins all over her, scurrying on over the branches.

'But stay close. And not all the way to the top. It's too dangerous. She nodded towards the pixies. 'And they are not coming!' They held their hands out at the unfairness. Then they shrugged and started sword fighting with pine needles on the bonnet of the car, aiming for each other's eyes.

'Deal!' said Poco, who bounded over and hugged her. 'Are you sure you don't want a lift?' he asked. He went back to the car and pressed down some sticky tape that was holding it together.

'No-one should go in that car. I am doing perfectly well on foot.' They looked up. It was as if the tree had grown more branches above them, the top nowhere to be seen. As the challenge ahead dawned on them, after a long awkward silence, Nell said 'Okay, let's get going.' She bit her lip. 'Someone told me she isn't real.'

'Only one way to find out,' he said, and held out his elbow for her to hold, which she did, relaxing again.

'Goodbye pixies! Behave yourselves.'

'To be honest, they are a liability,' said Poco under his breath as they set off. The pixies huffed, kicked the wheel back into place, and sped off in the Red Baron in the opposite direction.

CHAPTER 12

CAN YOU WISH FOR A WISH TO COME TRUE?

Far above them, Ava perched on a branch and watched out over the square, preening her feathers. Indy stood down below, keeping an eye on the crows. The friends reached the star garland Emma had brought, around halfway up the tree. In the square, occasional visitors hurried past. They stopped to admire the Christmas tree as they pulled their collars up against the cold. Hope hung in the air like a haze.

The pair continued onwards in each other's easy company. They passed a round shining silver bauble and made faces at each other in the reflection, laughing so hard that a crow flew off a nearby tree.

As they walked, Poco told Nell stories about his long life at Hawthorn House. He told her of kings and queens from the old days, even older than your parents. He talked about Christmas balls, like the one where the choir had awakened, at the end of yet another war. In those days, women wore huge impractical dresses and men wore curly wigs. When Nell stopped laughing, he recounted garden parties with jugglers and music and fascinating lectures from explorers and philosophers. Plays performed in round open theatres. A time where people were punished by having vegetables thrown at them in wooden stocks.

Nell told them of Emma's life, and her father in hospital. How since Bob's bookshop had to close, Emma's mother couldn't sleep at night, and how Emma kept Nell under her pillow. She told him about Mr Tribulus, and about the factory where Emma's mother was going to have to work, by Pewskbury sewage works. Poco was so angry he jumped up and down and started boxing the air, practicing what he might do to Mr Tribulus. Or at least what he might do to his ankle.

'I am sorry, Nell; I see why you awakened,' said Poco, putting his tiny hand on her shoulder.

'Well, we are putting it right.' She nodded decisively, the starlight of her soul burning brightly inside. The new friends looked out over the river, which shimmered with ribbons of orange evening sky, the north star now winking above them. A group of wooden animals bounded past, a squirrel, badger and an owl. A fox numin followed, stopped on the edge of the branch overlooking the square. She watched with big shining eyes as two real fox cubs played in the apricot glow of the empty square below. She bounded off after her friends. Nell pulled a seed from between the scales of a pinecone growing next to them and held it up.

'To think this whole tree was once a tiny seed just like that,' she said. They looked at the seed, then at each other. They linked arms and took in the beauty around them. When night drew in, they rested in a patch of moonlight, settling beneath the enormous branches that still dipped and curled above them. Nell pulled her arms around herself against the cold as the black night rolled in. Poco pulled down a fluffy snowball and snuggled into it; Nell followed suit.

The night was now strung with stars, and those strange green tinged clouds formed on the horizon again. Nell shivered.

'I wish it wasn't so dark,' she said, gazing up at the sky.

'Then we wouldn't be able to see the stars,' said Poco. He pointed out Orion, the Plough, The Milky Way, and other constellations drifting overhead as the earth slowly turned. They watched for shooting stars to make more wishes on and decided that a satellite would do.

'Can you wish for a wish to come true?' asked Nell. Snuggled together, each with the other's stories twirling through their minds, they slept.

In the town, a man checked his bank balance and chuckled to himself.

*

Dawn brushed her wings over the tree and ushered the dark away. Nell woke, refreshed and full of hope, to the sound of Poco snoring loudly. She giggled.

'Whatsatnoise?' Poco flapped his limbs about, looking all around him in a panic. 'What? Where? Oh.' He looked sheepish as he realised where he was. 'Oh, sorry.' Nell laughed so hard her tummy hurt. They fell into a giggling heap. A crow caw sliced through the morning silence as they set off.

A large striped hot-air balloon made from purple and gold silk carried numins up between the branches. Otto the nutcracker and Mick the post box stood in its basket and waved up to them. They waved back.

'We might as well go to this meeting. It looks like it's on our way.'

'It would be rude not to,' said Poco.

Dozens of numins flowed in one direction and the friends followed. Sprout had joined a group of frosted glass vegetables who jiggled along in a line on the branches below. A shimmering dark pink beetroot, a bright orange carrot and a broccoli stalk with a red chilli pepper. They bobbed alongside sheep, the penguins, the three plump geese and the sausage dogs. A llama with long, bright tassels walked in front of the wooden animals, with a cow wearing a Santa hat. The guinea fowl followed behind Kevin the hare, who was explaining the rules of sproutball. Dozens more flocked from all sides of the tree, headed in the direction of the fellowship gathering. The sloth had somehow caught up with them too and was sleepwalking, or rather, sleep-hanging, under the branch below them, with a tabby cat slinking behind. They travelled on in silence, and soon enough, they heard chattering voices up ahead.

CHAPTER 13

VASPAR AND THE SAUSAGE ROLL

'Let's keep a low profile,' said Nell, looking down into the clearing on the branch below.

'We should be careful.' Poco nodded. They lay down and peered through the needles to where the numins gathered. Poco pulled his cloak over his head and lay like a commando.

The branch below was wide, with glass baubles hanging from branches above, like great chandeliers. Someone had arranged lights and ribbons in loops around the edge of the space, so it looked like a town hall ready for a Christmas party. It was teeming with numins, talking, and exchanging stories. Some sat on Christmas crackers arranged like benches. Vaspar stood at the front. Nell's jaw clenched at the sight of him.

'I met him when I arrived. He really gave me the creeps.'

'He does seem to have something of the night about him,' said Poco, pulling his blanket further over his head. Nell's skin shivered.

Vaspar surveyed the crowd through narrowed eyes. There were more than a dozen nativity sheep, a goat, and the cow with the Santa hat. Bunnies with fluffy tails jumped around the mice with skis. The turtledoves settled near the geese, and the wooden animals who had passed them sat on top of a cracker in a row. The glass dragonfly flitted above the crowd. The angry Father Christmas was telling off the cat figure with a red bow who just licked his paw. Nearby a white pompom snowman and a pompom penguin with goggly eyes wobbled together. Otto the nutcracker and Mick the post box were chatting to the llama. Mick showed them how his letters worked as messages, and Otto demonstrated his strong jaw, snapping a twig in half. Ava perched on a branch near Ruby, who was tumbling around next to her, puffing deep purple sparks from her beak. Indy stood nearby, his head high. The vegetables jostled for space on a cracker next to Kevin the hare and Anka the polar bear bookmark. A large party of awkward looking beetles with dark knobbly backs and sharp pincers lined up around them.

'What are they?' said Poco, screwing up his face. Nell's toes curled.

'Death-watch beetles, I think.' She had seen a documentary about them with Emma. They gave her the creeps as much as Vaspar did. 'They kill things.'

Glacia stood behind Vaspar with the sugar-mice circling around her. Poco chuckled and nudged Nell. He pointed over to the pixies, who were hopping about pulling faces and blowing raspberries at everyone. Nell watched Vaspar through narrowed eyes, who was now tickling and patting a sheep, who giggled at the attention. Her stomach squirmed.

'So, this would be the fellowship.' She nodded as she viewed the gathering.

'We will hear what he has to say, then move onward if we want to,' said Poco. Nell gave him the thumbs up. Vaspar held his arms out wide. Silence trickled through the crowd and all eyes fell upon him.

'I'm sure that you are all wondering what my secret is!' He began.

'How I live, who I am, my philosophy of life.' He coughed into his hand for a long time. Nell and Poco looked at each other. A sea of blank numin faces stared at him, at each other, and then back at him. 'Welcome to the Hope's End Christmas Tree Fellowship!' He raised his arms high and closed his eyes, to deafening applause.

'At last, we have come together! Now it's time for change.' More clapping erupted from the numins. 'We can't keep on like this, can we?'

'We can't!' They chanted.

'It's too hard, isn't it? What's happening with the humans.' He walked up and down the stem between them as if on a stage.

'Too hard!' they cheered.

'Terrible!' said some.

'The problems of the town have thrown things into an ugly light.'

'So ugly!' The crowd chimed.

'So, given their shameful ruin, and their mistreatment of us, well, it is time for us to separate from them. Once and for all! Now we can form our own fellowship, just for us!' The crowd fell silent.

'That's not right,' said Nell, gripping the pine needles.

'That is not what any numin fellowship is about!' said Poco, glaring down at Vaspar.

'Do we want to be owned by the humans forever?' Vaspar continued, then, in a sing-song voice said: 'Go hang in the tree in the rain, they say. In the wind and cold, with the danger of the crows.' He shook his head. 'Enough!' As if on cue, a crow swooped by and sent a hanging bauble spinning and knocking into him. 'Pest!' He shook his fist and glared at it before turning back to the group. 'It's time we took action against these terrible tyrants. Leave them to their disease and destruction. What did they ever do for us?' Heat rose in Nell's chest.

'Tyrants?' said Poco. 'The humans are our friends!' He tightened his fists.

'They are,' said Nell, her eyes fixed on Vaspar.

'This Christmas is the final straw for me. And you?' He peered into the face of a small sheep. 'Is it the final straw for you?'

'Er, yesss–' she trembled. Many numins looked from one to another. Poco shook with rage.

'I can't believe this is happening,' he said. 'This is nothing like the old fellowship. We have always helped each other to help the humans. That is why we live, to make life easier! We should be coming together to help them find a way out of the crisis.' His voice was getting louder.

'Shh,' said Nell, putting her finger to her lips. 'We can continue up to the angel. She will help, I am sure of it.' But Poco carried on, standing up and flapping his arms around.

'He is using the crisis as a chance to gain power! I knew there was something fishy going on.'

'Let's go on up. The angel will be on our side,' said Nell, worry twisting inside.

'We can return to this. I see Ava and Indy over there. They will feel the same.' But Poco didn't stop.

'He's bonkers. I mean, the humans have loved us for hundreds of years. Thousands. They made us. That's literally why we exist!' He spluttered. 'We can't separate from them. We need each other. We would have no meaning in our lives. We would all die.' He became so upset that he lost his balance and fell through the branch onto the one below where the numins were gathered. He rolled in his cloak towards Vaspar's feet, where he landed with a bump, looking rather like a sausage roll.

CHAPTER 14

THE WORST IDEA, EVER

Nell gulped at the sight of Poco lying at Vaspar's feet. He looked as if he was now playing dead, which only made things worse. Nell cringed. Realising, rightly, that this was a bad idea, Poco stood up.

'Oh, heh heh,' he said, his cheeks a deep shade of raspberry. He stared right into the eyes of a death-watch beetle, who stood on his hind-legs and clicked his pincers at him. He backed away with his hands up. 'Hi everyone. Goodness me, I am a clot!' He looked up at Nell and pulled an apologetic face. Vaspar peered at him, then his puzzled eyes followed Poco's gaze up into the branch above, where Nell stood looking sheepish.

'Well, well, well.' Vaspar sneered, rubbing his

hands together.

'Oh, hello! Sorry we are late for the meeting. Ha ha! We just got here. So, anyway,' said Nell casually as she jumped down. 'Do carry on, don't mind us. Just passing by actually! Ha ha!' She wasn't very convincing.

'Nell. What a pleasure to see you again!' He grinned. 'Settle down, do. You are especially welcome.' He bowed, not taking his eyes off her. He turned to Glacia and said under his breath: 'No wonder Hope's End is in so much trouble! Perhaps we need an entry system.' He nodded towards Poco. Glacia, the sugar-mice, and the death-watch beetles sniggered.

'Oh Vaspar, stop it!' said Glacia, slapping his arm. Then she laid her icy eyes on Nell. A shadow crossed Nell's heart. Poco nestled himself between two plump geese nearby, who shuffled up and nodded warmly to him. He shook the tips of their wings with his tiny hands.

'Friends. We have new recruits!' said Vaspar. 'Now, perhaps we can iron out the details of the fellowship together. Nell is a new numin.' Some applauded. 'We know that having someone so fresh is an asset going forwards.'

'He is making it look like I am on his side,' said Nell in a low voice.

'So, we need rules! Firstly, everyone must arrive on time.' He looked at Nell again. 'Heh heh, just kidding!' His eyes bored into hers and she turned away. 'We will look at each other when we are speaking.' He stared with a twist of a smile. She pretended to look at the other numins. Indy moved closer to her, glaring at Vaspar.

'Good idea,' said Nell, regaining strength as Indy stood by her. She held his gaze. Vaspar turned back to the crowd.

'Next rule: No questions, unless they support the main view of the fellowship, let's not waste time.' A bunny, who had raised her paw to ask a question, pretended that she was stretching and put it back down.

'Your view more like,' said Nell under her breath.

'We are all equal here, especially me,' he said.

'And me!' said Glacia.

'Yes, and you, my little icicle,' he crooned. Nell felt sick. Poco grimaced.

'We have to get out of here,' she said.

'Just a moment,' Indy said, raising his head high and clearing his throat. There was a moment of silence, and all eyes were on him.

'I am Indy. They may be busy with other things for now, but our role is to help the humans. I will help mine for as long as I can. They don't show thanks, no. Because they do not know what we do for them. That's not the point. This is what a numin is. We are made, loved, and brought to life by humans. We only exist because of them. We are bound to them by souls. My friends here and I want to come together as a fellowship to help them, and each other, more, not less. To make friends, solve problems like the town crisis, together as one. Without our help, and this chance we have now, Hope's End could be doomed to misery forever, and you know it.'

'You are wrong,' said Vaspar. 'They are getting what they deserve with this sickness, the hopeless idiots! Let's leave them to it. This Christmas is our chance to end it all. End their control of us for thousands of years. It is time to escape. We won't need them; we can feed off each other's energy.' He looked at Nell for a long time, then coughed again. 'Numin groups have been known to live without humans in the past.' He grinned. Why was he looking at her? A shiver crawled down her back. Indy moved still closer to her. The crowd looked from one to the other. Some scratched their heads. Others whispered among themselves. Glacia and the pixies applauded. So did the miserable Santa. The sloth started to cry. Otto patted her shoulder.

'Don't worry, Ziggy,' he said in a gentle voice.

The death-watch beetles clapped their pincers. 'They aren't even numin!' said Nell, scrunching her face into a scowl.

Ava perched on a nearby branch and spread her wings wide. Her jet-black eyes glittered. Ruby, who had been sparking furious red since Vaspar started talking, settled next to her.

'I am Ava. My robin friend is Ruby. We agree with Indy. Numins live to inspire, to protect, to love. Life without them is meaningless. Parting from them will bring nothing but death to us, and I fear, to them too.'

Nell moved closer to the crowd, stood tall, and spoke in a clear voice.

'I only want to be a guardian to the humans, to

my human,' she said. 'I can't be part of this fellowship unless it is for them, too. We are stronger together. Who agrees?' A sea of arms shot into the air.

'I do!' bellowed Poco, one of the geese and several others. The bristling king trembled with anger, flakes falling off him.

'And us!' said the sausage dogs, penguins, and bunnies, and many more.

'I love my human!' yelled Otto with his arm in the air, his nutcracker jaw almost falling off.

'Look, mine knitted me this jumper on cocktail sticks,' said a mouse, 'and made our ski's.' She showed the crowd amidst mutters of 'lovely!' 'Such fine handiwork,' and 'beautiful stitching.' Vaspar rolled his eyes.

'Pathetic! They drain us of energy. They wear us out,' he said, pulling a loose flake off his cloak. 'And for what?' He coughed.

'For love, for comfort, for meaning?' said Ava. 'She flew and landed on Indy's antler, ringing softly as she did. Ruby tumbled over too and landed on a sprig of pine above Nell's head. Nell smiled at her. Poco stood up.

'I am never leaving Hawthorn House, or our caretaker,' he said, folding his arms. 'The humans need us. Did you know that if it wasn't for us, Guy Fawkes would have blown up Parliament that day? That was because my band and other numins stuck together!' He turned to one of the geese. 'He was a surprisingly quiet man, you know.'

'It looks like you are on your own, Vaspar,' said

Indy. 'Perhaps you need to review your plan.'

'I can see you need more time to let the idea sink in,' said Vaspar, eyeing him coldly.

'We have a chance for a new fellowship, disease free, stupidity free. Parties every night! Besides, the longer we stay with them, the more life they drain out of us. I am certain that we would all be dead by next Christmas at this rate if we stay.' Some of the numins gasped.

'I don't want to die!' said a sheep.

'Exactly. So, we will break off, save ourselves, and finally stop picking up the pieces of their stupidity.' He threw his arms open in a dramatic finale. 'And I volunteer myself to be your leader!' The death-watch beetles started clicking a deathly rhythm. They clicked next to the little sheep, bunnies, and sausage dogs, who trembled in fear. 'Clap then!' said Vaspar. The little creatures quaked and clapped while the other numins looked on. Vaspar tensed his arms, furious at the weak applause. 'If we stay as we are, then–' He pulled his fingers across his neck, making a cutting sound, then gazed at Nell with a stiff smile. More numins trembled.

'Nell, I hope you are convinced.' She could feel her cheeks burning as he focussed on her yet again. 'I will need, I mean, want, you on board.' She was about to speak when the pixies started hopping about and rhyming something to each other. Vaspar huffed and looked across at them and, still shaking, he boomed:

'No talking when I'm talking. Unless you share it with everyone.' They stopped rhyming. For the first time, a serious expression crossed their faces. 'Well? Please share your thoughts with the group,' he said, with the biggest and fakest smile yet.

'Heh heh. If I must!' said the taller pixie:

> *She seeks the angel at the top, she thinks the King is a stupid flop.*
> *It's home she wants, and she won't stop, convinced she is, he ain't much cop!*
> *Her friends agree, this is their tree, you need to change, or you should flee!*

'Hey!' said Nell. Laughter rippled through the crowd. 'That is not what I said, I–' She stopped herself. She couldn't deny it. She glared at the pixies.

'Such silliness. I am sure Nell thinks no such thing!' A few more flakes fell off his cloak as he shook with rage. He gave one of the pixies a slap on the back. The pixie fell flat on his face and ended up with a mouthful of needles. The other one pointed at his brother and fell about laughing. Glacia giggled into her hand. Vaspar's eyes bored into Nell's.

'The angel will never agree with you. I will talk to her about the town's problems too, and she will sort them out,' said Nell.

'Ha! Nell is a new numin, aren't you?' he said. 'You don't know what you are doing or saying yet! Any numin angel will be on my side, at my right hand. Such a magnificent asset deserves a place at my table! She won't like the tyranny of the humans any more than me. Why would she listen to a little new numin who doesn't know what she's doing?' He turned to the crowd. 'I do question, fellow numins, why Nell would want to travel all the way up to the top, just for a stupid girls wish. I wonder, is there something you're not telling us Nell? Some secret plan? Why on earth would she help you, anyway?' Nell straightened.

'Because she is strong and wise. And I am small, and kind and I want to help our humans,' she said, courage growing bright inside her. His face fell, astonished that someone so small and sweet could behave with such strength.

'Preposterous! She wouldn't have the time. These humans don't deserve angelic wisdom, anyway. They have blown it. They are being punished with this plague. Anyway, you will never make it up there! Especially not with this clown!' He gestured towards Poco.

'Hey!' said Poco. Nell forgot all the eyes staring at her and continued, shaking a little.

'I will go to the angel,' she said, 'and I will get Emma's wish answered. I will ask her to solve the town's crisis. Because that is why I am here. That is why I am a numin.' Poco clapped with all his might.

'Come back when you've finished, eh, Nell? We will be here when the angel sends you packing!' His lip curled into a sneer.

'The angel will stop you making everyone break away from human's, too. I'm going,' snapped Nell. Poco was already nodding goodbyes. Ava bowed to them and landed on a nearby branch. Poco saluted to his new geese friends, who saluted back. He bounded over and backflipped along the branch. He held his fingers up in a victory 'V' sign to the crowd. The geese made 'V' signs with their wing feathers, though low down and out of Vaspar's sight.

Nell turned back to Vaspar. 'This is the worst idea I've ever heard.'

'Boo hoo!' he said with a menacing gaze. 'Don't get angry when she doesn't help you!' He teased.

'I will never ever want to break away from the humans!' she said.

'Then you will never be part of this fellowship!' His words cartwheeled through her.

'Fine!'

Ruby accidentally let out a huge streak of orange fire in Vaspar's direction. She tried to hide her beak with her wing as he ducked.

'Watch out for things that go bump in the night.' He crept towards Nell. 'Gah!' He wiggled his crusty hands at her.

Nell's tummy lurched. She whipped around and stomped along the branch towards the trunk. The crowd watched, frozen and wide eyed. Were they so afraid of him? So afraid they might die in this crisis too? Nell and Poco plunged through the dark needles into the deep of the tree, where the branches were so gnarled and tangled that it was hard to get through. The thick needles scratched them, curling, and closing in on them. Nell held up Opus's staff. It glowed like a tiny sun. They followed the light.

CHAPTER 15

THE ANGEL

'Onwards!' hollered Nell. She pointed the staff towards the treetop, which sparked bright white. They squeezed their way upwards through the tangle of needles and tinsel, from branch to branch, as fast as they could. The branches became narrower as they climbed. Poco muttered a prayer to Saint Christopher.

'I can't stand all this stuff. It keeps getting in my eyes,' he said, pushing his way through the needles. 'But I love your courage, Nell!'

'I'm just following my heart.' She sounded more confident than she felt inside.

'Standing up to bully's is hard,' said Poco, looking at her with admiration.

'We can't let him win. Why would Vaspar hate the humans so much, anyway?'

'I think Vaspar is losing his life force because he is unloved,' said Poco. 'His body is failing. He thinks that breaking away from humans will solve it. But it is the opposite. It is the help we give that keeps us alive. 'He looked right into her eyes. 'Nell, it is possible that Vaspar wants a soul like yours. Be careful. Envy is a dark force.'

'So, if he loved or helped someone, it would save him?'

'Yes. To abandon the humans is to abandon all hope. We have seen it happen over the centuries.' He looked down and sighed. 'Tragic.'

'I am so glad you are here with me,' said Nell, her face blossoming into a smile.

'At your service!' said Poco, saluting, as he dangled from a red beaded thread.

Nell put Vaspar to the back of her mind as they climbed higher and higher. The branches became so tangled in places that they had to crawl on their hands and knees to get through. It seemed as if menace was under every needle, every bauble, and fluttering through every piece of tinsel. Each wondered if they would ever get there.

A twig snapped below. They stopped and looked at each other. Holding their breath, they turned and looked down. A death-watch beetle emerged from the dark and scuttled away.

'This tree just gets creepier and creepier,' said Poco, spitting out a pine needle. Each let out a long breath and carried on climbing. The further they travelled, the less certain Nell felt about anything.

'We should sleep now,' she said, yawning, as night drew in. 'Ready for the final push in the morning.' Poco nodded. They huddled together next to a grey velvet heart decoration and, exhausted, fell asleep, despite their worries.

*

A thin ray of sun broke through the pine needles and warmed Nell's face. The smell of early morning earth and pine laced the air. Nell tucked the staff into her jumper, and Poco pulled his blanket around him. Their noses and ears were cold and pink. They moved further into the inside of the tree as the branches thinned nearer the top, leaving the decorations, and wind, behind. Inside, bony branches jutted out from the trunk like a skeleton. The air was stale. Using the staff as a hook and helping each other, they made their way up. Their faces shone in its light. Nell wondered what Emma was doing now.

The branches soon became so spaced out they were impossible for Poco to climb. The trunk narrowed, and the branches formed a natural spiral staircase to the top. It was like climbing the stairs inside an old church spire, with an apprehensive feeling to match. A glint of gold winked far up above them in the light. Nell's tummy flipped.

'Look,' she said, tugging Poco's arm. They peered

up, wide eyed. Shards of gold light dappled onto them, as bright as hope.

'It must be the angel!' said Nell, her tummy a tangle of knots.

'You will have to do the last bit alone,' said Poco, pulling his cloak around himself so only his face peeked out.

'What if I don't make it? What if she isn't alive? What if she is on Vaspar's side? What if—' Her tummy was doing somersaults.

'Then, we are doomed,' said Poco, shrugging. Nell's face fell.

'Only joking!' Poco nudged her. She elbowed him.

'Don't tease!'

'You will be fine. We all believe in you. Just deliver the wish and take it from there. I'll be right here. You can do it,' said Poco with a warm smile.

'Tally ho!' She held the staff high, which glowed bright white. With an unsteady hand, she reached up and grabbed the short, needly branchlets that stuck out from the trunk. She climbed and climbed, leaving Poco clinging below, his face peering up at her.

An eerie wind picked up and whistled through the pine needles. The gold glints dimmed as dark clouds obscured the sun, and the wind bent the trunk from side to side. It groaned and creaked. A garland of shimmering gold honesty seeds looped around the short branches started to swing. Crows cawed in the distance. Tiny bright lights appeared, zipping around her like fireflies, stinging her.

'Ow!' She pulled her staff out. 'Get off! I am on

an important mission!' She swiped at them, then held the staff high, tightening her hand around it.

'No flies, please!' The baton blazed deep orange and the little lights twitched and flew away. She took a few steadying breaths, and the angel came into view above her. Nell gasped; her eyes fixed on her. The whispering winds turned to howls as heavy raindrops splatted onto her like huge tears from the sky. 'It's just a passing storm,' she said to herself, trying to stay calm. Gales replaced the winds, and the rain fell harder. 'Emma, I'm nearly there!' She spluttered through the rain, her heart thundering. 'Everything will be fine!' She slipped as the needles spiked her. Steadying herself, she clamped onto the spindly trunk beneath the angel. The air smelt electric. Nell's stomach clenched.

She glanced up. The angel was made of gold stiff metal. Her long golden hair flowed rigidly down her back. Her white decorated wings ascended far above her, studded with jewels. Her halo hung like a stiff vine above her head. Her face was white, her eyes fixed, staring blankly out. Vacant and lifeless. Tears stung Nell's eyes. Burning with desperation, she took a deep breath, and spoke with a wavering voice.

'Your Majesty.' Silence. Nell blinked away tears. The angel swayed back and forth in the wind. Drenched, she wiped her cheek with the back of her hand. The storm roared around her, the sky black in the daytime. Below, the decorations lurched in the gale. Numins far below ran for cover as the rain lashed against the tree. And then, the truth. The angel had a barcode sticker beneath her wings. Nell wept; her tears mixed with the rain. She knew it was no use but carried on. 'Angel, please answer Emma's wish! Please stop Mr Tribulus. Help them to stay in Hope's End. And the fellowship–, the town, Vaspar–' a fire of shame swept through her. 'What am I doing?'

The top of the tree bent right over in the tempest. The angel swung wildly forward, and Nell almost lost her balance. One gust away from doom, she wrapped herself around the spindly trunk with her whole body and looked down. Far below, people rushed inside their tiny houses, as tiles blew off the rooves. A man shoved his broken, upturned umbrella into a rubbish bin in the square. A bauble blew off the branch next to her and crashed down to the ground. Hundreds of other decorations followed. Dogs barked and howled to each other. A crack of lightning struck on the other side of the river. A clap of thunder rocked the air soon after. The numins shouting to each other for help as they dashed about in panic. Vaspar was in the meeting place, barking orders, pointing in all directions. A crow circled in the sky above as fear swept through her like the wild wind. A powerful gust caught underneath the angel and snapped her tether clean in two.

'Oh no!' She closed her eyes. Her mind filled with tangled thoughts. The lightning struck the church weathervane by the square, not far from her. Deafening thunder shook the angry sky. The numins below looked up. Nell opened her eyes again and watched in horror as another blast took the angel into the air and sent her sailing down into the river below. Fear blazed through her as she heard the distant splash. She stared down at the ripples on the surface, her eyes blurred with tears. The gold figure sank down, deep into the murky water and out of sight.

'She wasn't real! I left Emma for nothing!' She clung on to the swaying treetop, her wet cheek squeezed against the prickly stem as she searched for answers. One thought curled out from the tangle of her mind and hit her like a crashing cymbal. 'Unless–' Everything seemed to stop for a moment. Her chest swelled, and suddenly it was clear. 'I must do it myself!' The familiar starlight sparked inside her. 'I must stop Tribulus making them leave. The wish was meant for me!' The challenge of it dawned on her as she searched for courage within. Numins moved around lower down. 'Oh, boy do I need the fellowship's help!' she said when she spotted them. But there was Vaspar in the middle, staring up at her clinging to the treetop where the angel once stood. Nell and Vaspar's eyes caught each other. His face was horrified, accusing. He pointed his finger towards her. Nell's courage faded as dread tumbled through her. Her tummy flipped. Vaspar and the numins looked at her as if she was a criminal. She clutched the top of the tree in place of the angel.

'Oh no!' she breathed. 'No!'

CHAPTER 16

NELL'S CHOICE

Nell's legs wobbled as she climbed down, the storm raging around her. She wiped tears from her cheeks with the back of her hand.

'Great. No angel! I have been on a pointless mission, and I failed. Nice work, Nell. Vaspar was right, I don't know what I am doing.' She clambered back down through the chaos, shaking with despair. Pieces of smashed, tangled decorations lay everywhere, on and off the tree. When she got down, Poco wasn't there. She snorted. 'And my only friend left me. That's just blinking fantastic. What am I supposed to do?'

She moved down through the empty middle of the swaying tree. It was like an enormous creepy climbing frame, without the fun. The tempest quietened, leaving an earthy scent in the air. Glimmers of sky outside the tree changed from black to grey. Her breathing steadied. She peered down through the branches. Where is Poco? Does he think I pushed her off too?' Her lip trembled. 'And the first sign of madness is talking to yourself. Great.' Tears pricked the back of her eyes. 'I have to get home to Emma. I must think of a way to stop Tribulus before it's too late.' She gulped. 'Right now.'

Something strange caught her eye on a branch on the other side of the trunk. Through the murk of the tree, he appeared to be a grubby brown figure, not much larger than Nell. He wore grimy brown clothes, as if he had been living in the mud since the dinosaurs. His face was smudged with dirt. He lay still, but there was something else. The sound of tapping. Tap, tap. Tap, tap. Marching death-watch beetles. Two by two along the branch towards him, pincers raised and snapping. Nell put her hands to her face.

'Hey! Hey you!' she shouted. Her voice echoed through the space of the tree to the still figure. 'Oi, you! Get up! The beetles are coming after you! They are going to hurt you!' No movement. He had a little bag with him. A snatcher, perhaps. She paused for a moment, then grabbed a piece of bark from the trunk and threw it at him. It missed. She tried again. This time, it hit.

'Ow!' He opened his eyes and blinked around him, the whites of his eyes showing as he saw the beetles approach. One started pinching at his foot, and another came up the other side, tugging at his leg. Then he met Nell's eyes.

'Help!' he groaned. He tried to drag himself away, but he was too slow. The beetles kept coming, nipping at his feet. A snatcher maybe, but a snatcher in trouble. 'Please help me!'

'Coming!' She hopped down over the branches towards him. Then she remembered Emma, and Mr Tribulus. Time was running out. She stopped. If she made it outside, even if she didn't find Poco, she could slide down the tinsel to the ground and be home by evening. A plan would occur to her on the way. At the very least she would be with Emma before they left town, even if she failed to stop Tribulus. She looked at the limp figure, knowing she had to leave him if there was any chance to get home and complete the wish. Someone else will help him, surely. The two choices battled with each other in her mind. She had to go to Emma. It was her only chance.

'Sorry,' she called behind her as she turned. 'I'm sure you'll be alright. I have to go. I really am sorry.' She tried to push down the guilt that choked in her throat and ran out along the branch towards the gloomy daylight.

'Please!' said his small, still voice from far behind her. She stopped again and sighed. Of course he wouldn't be alright. There was no one else around. He would die, alone. And it would be because of her. Emma would help him. She thought of her friends, the help the choir gave her without question when she arrived, and Indy, and Ava. The risk Poco took to come with her. Tears filled her eyes again, but so did determination.

'Talk about timing. Hold on!' She turned and started back across the branches towards him. The beetles were now pinching at his legs, and one had crawled up to pinch his side. He tried to crawl away. Nell passed a spider and had an idea. She knew that spiders liked to eat beetles from the documentary she saw with Emma. 'Oh, Mr spider, I have something for you. Look over there! Suppertime!' The spider saw the beetles and scurried along the branches towards them. He made a gleeful chittering sound, and more spiders followed from the shadows. The deathly drumming rang out. It sounded like 'Kill him! Kill him!'

Nell's heart pounded. She pushed fear to one side. When you know you are doing the right thing, everything feels easy. Her body strengthened as she bounded from branch to branch with ease. When she was near, she pulled out the staff and held it tight. It fizzed with an eerie blue light and startled the beetles backwards. She batted the stubborn ones away, and the chittering spiders followed them. She helped the figure up.

'This way.' Nell pulled her arm around him, under his armpit, and helped him away along the branches. The beetles retreated with the spiders close behind. She hoped he was worth it.

CHAPTER 17

THE SNATCHER

He had bright, clever eyes and a kind face. His clothes were grubby, his face was smeared with grime. Though she wasn't exactly the picture of tidiness, especially after her time on the tree.

'What happened to you? Where did you come from?' she asked, working hard not to wrinkle her nose in front of him.

'It's a long story,' he said with a wide, weary smile. 'I am a bit of a lurker, I suppose, ha! I've been living in this tree for a while.' He pushed the strap of his bag up over his shoulder. 'Then these charming creatures showed up and, well, they didn't like my face I guess.' He smiled from under the smudges.

'Ah, was it you we heard lurking in the branches as we moved up the tree earlier? We thought it might be a snatcher!'

'I am a snatcher.' He pulled an apologetic grin. Nell gulped. Had she just saved a snatcher rather than go home to Emma? 'Thank you for saving me. I thought I was a goner!'

'Don't mention it.' She felt queasy. They settled on a soft young branchlet with bright green needles while he got his strength back.

'I've been living with the crows. I snatch for them.'

'The crows? That isn't much better.' She frowned unable to ignore a sinking feeling inside.

'It's not what you think!' He held up his hands to her. 'I only take unwanted items. Crusts from picnics, for example. From litter bins, pockets. And now, Christmas trees. Never numin. Just things people don't want that it's difficult for the crows to get. I am a numin,' he said, 'honest.'

'Don't you have an owner? A home?'

'I do. I did anyway.' He looked at the ground. 'That's another story. I'm sorry, it's complicated!' He shrugged and rubbed his wounded side.

'Sorry, I was just curious. You need to heal. Can I help? I am glad you are safe now.' She looked into his eyes. They sparkled, though a troubled expression crossed them.

'I must go. Thank you for saving me. Those beetles are horrible once they get a sniff of you.' He stood up, holding his hand against his injured side. 'I will tell you more another time if I see you again. The crows, well, they are tricky. And they have something nasty up their sleeve. I really must leave, thank you.'

He smiled at her. 'You're a rare gem!' She blushed. He jumped down through the branches as if he had done it all his life.

'Wait!' She hurried after him. 'What's your name? How did you get there in the first place?' But he pushed his way through the needles, and they closed behind him. Nell looked at the space he had bounded through, her mind filled with questions.

'Nell! Down here!' She spun around. A familiar voice echoed in the space. Poco looked up at her from a branch far down below, his bright eyes shining through the shadows.

'There you are! I thought you had left me!' she said.

'Never! I had an accident, but I'm fine.' Poco said, rubbing the top of his head. He had a black eye and a broad smile.

'Falling is fun!' said Poco. A problem with some flickering lights in the storm, that's all. Just a minor electrocution or three.' He laughed. 'Very refreshing! Now, how did it go? Did you get the answers, is the angel on our side, problems all solved are they?' His kind eyes gazed steadily at Nell. Her pale face said it all. She made her way down, though couldn't yet find any words. Tears welled in her eyes as her friend came close. The thought of failing Emma, of losing her wouldn't leave her. They hugged for a long time, then sat down together.

'The angel is just a fancy ornament. Glacia was right. She fell off and everyone saw and thinks I pushed her. They hate me. Vaspar thinks I am after some kind of glory. I just want things to be back the way they were, for Emma.' She buried her face in her hands, then took a deep breath and looked into Poco's warm, shining eyes. He wiped a tear from her face. 'Vaspar started saying things about me and pointing. They all looked so angry. I've failed and let everyone down. I'm going back to find Emma before she leaves if they haven't already gone. It was me who should have stopped Mr Tribulus all along. And now it's too late.'

'Oh, of course the wish was meant for you, why didn't I think of it? We will come up with something. Have faith. It's not over yet,' Poco nudged her. 'We can clear your name and stop Vaspar messing things up. No angel, eh? Opus will be disappointed.' Nell's lip wobbled.

'So far today I have led my friend to be electrocuted. I've killed everyone's hope of an angel, possibly even killed an angel, everyone thinks so.' She flapped her arms around. 'I may have broken the bond with my human by accident, and the fellowship is a mess and hate me. Oh, and by the way, I saved a snatcher, too. Just put that one on the list. The other numins are hardly going to rally round to help me after all that, are they? I'm just about the worst thing on this tree.' She slumped onto the branch. 'I failed Emma, you, and everyone else. And I don't know what to do.' She sniffed. 'But I have to try.' Poco crouched down next to her.

'Perhaps it's not been the greatest day of your life,' he said, patting her shoulder.

'That doesn't make me feel a whole lot better,' said Nell.

'Just saying,' Poco shrugged. 'You helped a snatcher?' he asked.

'Yes. Don't worry, he went that way.' She lowered her eyes.

'It's fine, Nell. The answers will come. Our caretaker at Hawthorn House says we should make several small mistakes, at least three medium and one or two large mistakes every day,' said Poco, 'so we learn.' The corner of her mouth curled into a reluctant smile. She jumped up and hugged him.

'Thank you. I must be a genius now!'

'Me too!' said Poco. They laughed. 'This will pass. You'll see.' Poco held Nell's hands in his. 'You stood up for the fellowship and that counts for everything. It is wonderful that the numins found each other on this tree. Let's keep it that way.'

'I can't have everyone hating me.' She looked out towards the town, feeling stronger again. 'And I need help with Mr Tribulus. I don't know where he is or how to find him, or what I would do if I did. And maybe my bond with Emma is broken.' She stood up. 'All I know is, I am not ready to give up and let them go to Pewskbury and for Tribulus to win.'

'Reporting for duty!' Poco saluted. Warmth flowed through her at the sight of him. They travelled in the direction of the fellowship meeting place.

'The fact is greedy people will stop at nothing. They have no sense of enough,' said Poco, turning up his palms as they walked. He stopped, a thoughtful expression crossing his face. He turned to Nell. 'Sometimes we can change things and people like that when–'

'When–?' asked Nell, her breath light.

'Occasionally someone like that could change if–' He looked out to the sky.

'If–?' She twisted her braid around her hand, her eyes bright with hope.

'Well,' he looked right at her. 'If we can get right into their heart.'

'Their heart?' asked Nell, her own heart flickered.

'Yes. Their heart,' said Poco. He took both of her hands in his.

'Tribulus has a heart?' Nell blinked at him.

'Somewhere, deep down. Deep, deep, deep down. But he has forgotten it. If somehow, we can get to it, well, the answer will be there.'

'Well, how do I do that?'

'Oh, Nell, if I knew I would tell you, ha!' he said. 'I really have no idea! Right! Let's get moving!' He clapped his hands together and wandered along the branch towards the daylight. We are off to see Vaspar and the others, to clear your name, right?' Nell stared blankly after him.

*

They were now skilled at climbing and soon arrived near where the fellowship had met before. They hid behind some pine fronds and glanced around for Vaspar.

'There.' She pointed through the needles. Vaspar

stood with some numins sitting in front of him. Several sheep, the vegetables apart from Sprout, and the angry fake Santa, the bunnies, penguins, the guinea fowl, and the pincushion hedgehog. The glimmering petrol lizard darted across the space and away. Vaspar was talking, and they looked at him, some yawning. The bunnies were holding their eyes open. There were dozens of death-watch beetles lined up in rows around them. Nell heard rustling behind them.

'Dear friends!' A voice like an untuned harp chimed out. They swung around to see Glacia and her sugar-mice. Nell eyed her, shrugged, and turned back towards Vaspar. Many thoughts and feelings raced through her mind. That Glacia had been right. The angel wasn't real, and Nell chose not to listen. Even so, she didn't want to waste any more time on her.

'Would you dears come and help me with something? Some decorations have smashed in the storm and look rather frightening. Little Tabitha cut her paw on one.' The sugar-mouse held up her paw and whimpered. 'Will you help me gather the glass fragments? Let's make it all lovely again, hmm?' She batted her eyelashes. 'Please, it won't take a minute.'

'I'm staying here,' said Nell, trying not to roll her eyes. Poco breathed in the cool peppermint scent that hung in the air.

'Alright,' he said. 'But only for a moment. Nell, I'll will be back in a minute.' Looking at Nell, he pointed two fingers at his eyes, then at hers, and back again as he walked away backwards. Nell smiled. He followed Glacia through the branches. Nell watched Vaspar, who crouched down over a sheep that lay in front of him, trembling.

'Now, pay attention, everyone. Let me show how to deconstruct the problematic part of a numin. Some do become rather difficult, like this poor lost soul who disagreed with me earlier. But it's easy to fix. We don't want bad behaviour. It will prevent growth in our fellowship, won't it?' He turned and looked at them all. 'Won't it!'

'It will!' they said. The turtledoves, who had their wings folded, watched from a distance. The miserable Santa watched with interest.

'This method will make then better fellowship members.' He held something in his hand close to his body, in a way that hid it from everyone's view. Many peered in to get a closer look, including Nell. He raised his arm.

'Let's begin!' The little sheep lying in front of him quaked and spoke.

'Oh, I'm not so sure. I won't do it again, whatever I did. I will stop. Please let me go,' she whimpered. 'Was it because I spoke? Because I won't do that again. No, sir!'

'No need to doubt little one.' Vaspar tickled her under the chin. 'We will heal you, forgive you, and move on.' He smiled his joyless smile and raised his chin up high. The sheep blinked at him.

'What is he doing to that poor creature!' muttered Nell, heat rising in her chest. Some numins looked away in fear, others were delighted by the show. Another sheep scurried over and stroked the first one's hoof.

'There is no need for sympathy. A waste of time!' He stared at the second sheep then batted it away with the back of his hand. 'Away.' The sheep rolled over to the fake Santa, who huffed. She hid behind him.

'Perhaps you next?' He smiled after her. She covered her face with her hoof. 'Now.' He brought the object Nell couldn't quite see and held it up to the sheep's head. The sheep's eyes widened, the whites shining in fear.

'What are you– I can't stand by and watch this!' Nell looked around. Poco still hadn't returned. She pushed her way through the branches anyway and ran towards him.

'Leave her alone!' she said. Vaspar spun around.

'Well, well, well, the wanderer returns.' He stared at her as if he had daggers in his eyes. A slow smile appeared across his face, and he placed the object back into his pocket.

'I hoped we might bump into each other again, Nell. How lovely to see you! Enjoy your little adventure, did you, angel killer?' The numins gasped. The death-watch beetles turned, raised their pincers up and marched towards her.

CHAPTER 18

THE DEATH-WATCH BEETLES

'Let her go!' said Nell, pointing at the trembling sheep. She stood strong, though her legs were quaking. She clasped Opus's staff in her hand. Vaspar looked at her with sharp, steady eyes. The beetles circled her; pincers raised. The other numins shuffled awkwardly. The little sheep saw her chance and scurried to her friends, whimpering. Vaspar glared at Nell.

'It wasn't what you thought, up there,' she said, nodding up toward the treetop. 'The angel blew off in the wind. She wasn't real. She had a barcode. She was lifeless. It was a coincidence. I want everyone to know.'

'A coincidence! Are we expected to believe that! You standing up there at the top of the tree waving your little stick about? At the same moment the angel falls to her death? You knew she would side with me, so you pushed her. You wanted to take her place. You wanted power! I knew you were up to something from the very beginning.' Some of the numins gasped. 'Well, it won't work.'

'That's ridiculous and you know it.' She trembled with rage. 'All I want is to help Emma and her family, and the town if I could. Power is what you want. Most numins help make their families and friends lives better. Just because you don't care, and no-one cares about you, you want to ruin it for everyone,' she yelled.

'False and irrelevant! Fellows, not only does she want power, to kill angels, and to disrupt our fellowship. There is something else you should know about Nell.' They all looked at her.

'What?' she said, a hollowness creeping through her. He shot her a cruel smile.

'She is a snatcher.' He folded his arms and held his chin up. The numins gasped.

'What?' They looked at her, aghast. 'A snatcher? Nell?' said the angry Santa in disbelief. The lizard scurried past, shaking her head.

'Of course! Look at her!' She looked down at herself, covered in smudges and grime from climbing. Her hair was a mess. 'I saw her the other night, sneaking around on the tree, looking for swag.'

'No! I came to visit the angel.' Her body froze. 'You know that.'

'This is not yours.' He pointed at Opus' staff. 'You've stolen that, haven't you?'

'No, I haven't! I was given it. By a friend,' she pleaded. She glanced around for Poco for backup, but they still weren't back.

'Given it! Ha!' he laughed. 'I have heard that one before.'

'It belongs to a musician called Opus.'

'Well, where is this Opus?' He peered around with his arms stretched out, a wide grin across his crackled face. No one spoke. 'What a surprise! He isn't here, and no one seems to believe you! We will find it and take it back to him, poor thing, he must miss it. It looks special.' He wrenched it from her.

'Ow!' she said, rubbing her hand. 'Give it back!'

'This is what the fellowship is for,' he said. 'To put things right.' He stroked the tip of Opus' star with his fingertip. It gave him an electric shock and turned a dull grey. He winced though tried to hide it, and looked back to Nell. 'And of course, you tried to snatch the angel, too. You can't deny it. We saw you. This fellowship doesn't want numins like you in it, Nell. Nor your little friend.'

'What friend?'

'Your little grubby snatching buddy. Smudgy Smudgerson! Glacia saw you. Your dirty friend, who you helped. He is, isn't he? A snatcher I mean.' He leaned toward her and stared into her eyes.

'No, I don't know him I–'

'Ha! You would help someone for no apparent reason?'

'Well, yes, anyone would, I–'

'Save it.' He held up his hand and turned to the crowd. 'She is a snatcher!' He pointed at her. The numins gasped and covered their mouths. Four beetles grabbed her arms and held her. Nell's face flamed red as she struggled against them. She scowled at Vaspar.

'I am not a snatcher, and you know it,' she spluttered, rage and fear spiralling through her. 'You just want to get rid of me because I don't like your plan.' She twisted and turned to try to get away.

'Look, she's like a wild animal!' He pointed at her. 'Don't worry, you will be safe now, everyone. There will be no more snatching attempts on this tree,' he said to the aghast numins. Even the crows seemed to swoop in and caw accusations at her. 'Take her to the birdcage!'

'The what?' said Nell. The beetles closed in around her. She looked around for Poco. Anyone who might help, an idea, an escape. Where was he? The miserable fake Santa glared at her. The sheep, bunnies and geese cowered together. The turtledoves had flown away. Dozens more beetles came up behind her and tipped her onto her back. She struggled, terror tearing through her like lava. With Vaspar leading, they carried her off toward the dark inside of the tree.

'Help!' she yelled. 'Where are you taking me? You can't do this!' she cried. The tap-tapping of the beetles' feet sounded like rhythmic funeral drums.

CHAPTER 19

THE BIRDCAGE

They marched Nell to the dark side of the tree. She was hot with anger on the outside, though despair swirled inside. They travelled for what seemed an eternity along dying branches inside the tree, covered in cobwebs and dirt. They came to a golden birdcage which hung from a gnarled branch, with icy water dripping from it. The ground was far below. Ornate patterns decorated the gilded cage. It creaked as it rocked; the sound pierced the iron-cold air. The beetles carried her along and turned her to a standing position as she tried to break free. They held her in the doorway. Vaspar leant close to her ear.

'It isn't power I want; it is something much more interesting,' he said. Nell struggled against the beetles. He reached into his pocket and pulled out the object, a small orb like a marble. Swirls of light and dark spiralled inside the sphere. He held it up in front of her eyes. She gulped. A sickly smile flickered on his face. He whispered a spell. A bitter pain shot through her head and heart, followed by a flash of light that passed between her eyes and the orb. She blinked and staggered back into the cage. Her face paled to the colour of snow. Then, she felt as if nothing had happened.

'What have you done to me?' she said, drawing away from him.

Vaspar put the orb back in his pocket and slammed the cage door shut. The sound rang in her ears. She held her hands to her face.

'Our little secret.' He winked. His black eyes shone. She shuffled to the back of the cage and steadied herself on its cold metal floor as it swung. 'You will remain here until the end of your sentence.' He turned his back to her and walked away along the nearest branch, and without turning around, said. 'And until my little prize takes effect.' He held up the orb before putting it back in his pocket. It now had a transparent wisp of gold curling through its centre.

'For what? It's not fair!' Vaspar strutted into the distance, his beetles following behind him.

'Life isn't fair,' he chided over his shoulder. The sound of drumming died away. Nell was left alone.

Perhaps she could escape. She just couldn't see how, not yet. She tried the bars and the lock, but it was no use. The birdcage squeaked as it dangled. The end of a string of fairy lights crackled and sparked nearby like an angry snake. The space around felt like a cave in everlasting night. She jumped at every sound she heard. Cold seeped into her core, and she shivered constantly. She wrapped her arms around her knees, resting her chin on top of them. Wind moved the branches occasionally, revealing slivers of fading light outside the tree. Was it the end of Christmas eve already? The emptiness enveloped her like a cloak as she fought back tears. For a while, she gave in to complete hopelessness.

Emma's home would normally be strewn with wrapping paper and ribbons now, as piles of presents appeared under the tree. A soft white feather twirled in through the bars in the wind. Nell used it to cover her body. Eerie night-noises filled the air as darkness wrapped around her. She settled under her feather and pulled it up to her chin. A distant owl hooted.

Time either flowed quickly or slowly, with nothing in between. Her heart ached for Emma, her new friends, and the home she knew. *Prepare for the worst, hope for the best*, Emma's mother would say.

'Then I shall live here.' She nodded her head and admired the pretty golden colour of the birdcage, its elegant shape, and interesting markings. It was quiet, at least. She used the feather to brush out the dust and debris. She shook the bars of the door once more, but it was hopeless. *The sky is always blue, and the sun is always shining*, Emma's mother would say when Emma was gloomy. *Just wait for the clouds to pass*. She remembered the grand parties that Poco described, full of fun and life. She danced around her cage, pretending she was there. She sang and danced. Then she collapsed and cried until she felt empty.

Exhausted, she slept.

Soon after she had a strange dream. In the dream, the sun shone brightly in her eyes. Then she saw Emma and her mother standing in the doorway of their home with bags. Emma started dancing. Nell's soul filled with a new, powerful glow which woke her from the dream, just like the starlight surge she had in her awakening. The starlight faded and she rubbed her eyes and looked out into the emptiness around her.

Her mind tumbled back to Glacia's words. Perhaps Emma did not need her now. It was meant to be. Perhaps Pewksbury would be a great adventure for Emma, even if it was a bit whiffy. It probably isn't suitable for a tiny numin figurine, especially not one who is a massive failure. Some numin must find a different way to live, Glacia had said. She remembered Opus's words: not all numins have happy lives. She rested her forehead against the bars and looked towards the ground.

'I am so sorry, Emma!' Her words echoed around the darkness as a tear dropped from her eye, down through the empty space and out of sight.

CHAPTER 20

THE ORB OF SOUL ESSENCE

After Vaspar left Nell in the birdcage, he emerged out of the light side of the tree. The death-watch beetles scurried down the trunk and left him alone. He blinked into the setting sun. It blazed out over the river, a fat gold sphere of flaming power fighting the night. The sky swirled with pink and green clouds that turned orange at the edges. Pink flickers of sunlight played on the water, though he did not notice. He sat on a branch next to some golden Diya lights from Diwali. Taking the orb out of his pocket, he held it up to his eyes. He didn't notice the key to Nell's cage falling onto the branch behind him, or Opus's staff next to it. He gazed into the whirling wisps in the sphere.

'Freedom from death at last!' He held it close to his eyes and looked through. The gold wisp and flickers of the orb danced inside with the setting golden sun behind. Sunlight passed through from one side lighting up the cloudy substance within, his eyes on the other. He held it steady. A flash burst out and turned his eyes gold for a moment, a powerful glow surging through him, sparkling in his heart. The image of a girl came into his mind, dragging a suitcase across a hallway.

'Oh, no, what is this?' He shook his head and tried to back away. 'No, this isn't–' He held his head and rubbed it, as if something was there that shouldn't be. 'No, this isn't what I wanted, I–' Then, an unfamiliar rush of love sprinkled through him like sparkles of starlight. Starting from his eyes, they spread through his body and into his heart. He couldn't fight it, although at first, he tried. Something he hadn't felt for a long time. Tears filled his eyes, followed by calm. He felt tingling and prickling all over, and the faint beat in his chest he knew before grew stronger. The orb stopped glowing, and he put it back in his pocket. He held his hand to his heart and a peaceful smile crossed his face.

The sun's yolky evening glow dropped more shimmering bands of pink and amber light on the water. Swans, pink in the light, flew south, their flapping wings breaking the silence. His heart swelled at the sight.

'Beautiful,' he said. It was as if he saw everything for the first time. He stood up and glanced down to the square, straightening his cloak. He slid down a trailing piece of ribbon.

'I must pay my owner a visit! Wheee!' he laughed as he fell on the branch below in a heap. He slid down again and again, on ribbons and tinsel; down and down. Someone had been watching from the shadows and grabbed the key and Opus's staff where he had left them, before disappearing again, the staff now glowing red. Vaspar plucked a chocolate coin from the tree, slid down a last strand of tinsel, and hopped onto the ground.

He ran across the empty square, bathed in the pink evening light. A woodlouse wandered in front of him and tripped over onto its back, wriggling his legs in the air. Vaspar turned it over and waved as it scurried away. He ran to the man on the bench, asleep under his newspaper. Vaspar tossed the chocolate coin to him. The man lifted his head and saw the coin in the middle of his paper. He looked about and scratched his head. Vaspar had already hurried onwards. The man opened it up and ate the chocolate before lying back down again. Vaspar sped across the cobbles and out of the gap in the yew hedge into the darkness of the town.

CHAPTER 21

RUBY'S CARGO

Crows cawed, breaking the clanging silence within the tree. It was still dark though she hadn't been able to sleep. Nell used her feather to sweep out the dust and fallen needles again. Her mind was blank except for the tiny flame of hope she held, deep down. Then, on the other side of the space in the dim far side of the tree something caught her eye. Something gold moving and flapping around. Nell stood up and held the cold bars in her hands, not taking her eyes off it. The gold object became larger as it drew closer. Was that singing? Her heart jumped. She sang back. It exploded in a rainbow of sparks.

'Ruby!' Her face bloomed into a wide smile. Ruby flew up to the bars and fluttered on the spot. 'Oh, Ruby I am so pleased to see you!' Joy sparkled through her as spots of light rained over her. 'I am stuck!' She shook the bars. 'Oh, I was so hopeless, I should have had more faith someone would come!' She cried tears of relief as she put her arms out through the bars and stroked Ruby's scaly back. Loneliness shrank away and warmth filled its space. 'How did you know I was here?' Nell shook at the bars of the door again. 'It's locked,' she said. Ruby looped in somersaults, singing brightly and bobbed her head downwards. 'What? What is it?' asked Nell, puzzled. And then she saw it. A key tied to Ruby's leg. 'You clever thing! Where did you get this?' Ruby sang something and pointed outside with her wing, sparking red. She landed on top of the birdcage and poked her leg down through the bars. Nell reached up and untied the key. She put it in the lock and the cage door flew open. 'Thank you, Ruby!' Ruby showered her with a rainbow of sparks before she flew off, singing and diving out through the branches. Nell stepped through the doorway, which sent the cage swinging. 'Whoops!' She was free. Excitement bubbled in her chest as she jumped out and climbed onto the branch. She sped out along it, out to find her friends.

She ducked around and underneath baubles, fairy lights and iced biscuits, and couldn't stop smiling. When she came to the outside of the needles dozens of crows swooped towards the tree. They pecked at the decorations, the ribbons, the ornaments, and the numins. She put her hand to her mouth and gasped. The tree was under attack.

CHAPTER 22

THE BATTLE OF THE CROWS

'Oh, no, not the tree. Not the town's beautiful Christmas tree!' Desperation streamed through her. She sprinted out to find Poco. The twisting black bodies of the crows filled the air, swooping against the decorations and numins across the entire front of the tree. Nell's heart dropped like a stone. The numins defended themselves and each other. Some ran for cover in the branches, fear etched on their faces. She looked for Poco, Indy or Ava, anyone she knew and trusted. Mick and Anka stood on a branch in the distance, Mick spitting letters out like arrows. Anka was swirling a star decoration around her head with her white paw to see them off. The pixies bounced on the end of a branch further along, taunting the crows. One crow pecked at a pixie and missed. The pair ran shrieking into the shadows of the tree. Nell never imagined she would feel so happy to see those Pixies. Another crow smashed baubles with his beak.

'Nell! Over here!' called a familiar voice from a nearby branch. Nell spun around. Indy ducked out of the path of a swooping crow and moved towards her. 'Glacia told us you had gone home to Emma!' Poco stood on Indy's back wearing his tartan cloak, standing tall like a Masai Warrior. He waved a long pine needle like a sword in one hand. In the other, he held a chocolate coin as a shield. Relief washed through her at the sight of her friends.

'Nell!' He waved. Nell pulled down a garland of holly and berries and swung across to reach them. Indy caught her on his back, and she hugged him and Poco tight.

'Where have you been? Glacia tricked me, and then you disappeared. We thought you must have gone to find Emma.' Ruby darted around in front of the crows to confuse them. She breathed balls of black fire at any that came close. 'The numins know you are innocent. We told them what really happened, some anyway. Vaspar has disappeared.'

'Where were you then?' asked Indy and Poco at the same time, concern written on their faces.

'I was in a bird cage. I'll tell you about it later.' They stared at her, before the three ducked out of the way of a crow. 'What's happening here?' She didn't want to talk about her failure.

'They just started attacking,' said Poco. 'We don't

have a clue why.'

'Let's put a stop to it. We can't have the tree ruined. That would just about finish this town! Their Christmas gathering tomorrow morning will be a disaster. All their treasures damaged, on top of everything else. So much for a symbol of hope!'

'What about Emma?' asked Indy. 'Poco said the angel wasn't real. That you are going to fulfil the wish yourself.' He looked at her with an admiring smile. 'But you can't go home now.' A crow swooped through the fog and carried a sheep off in its beak, dropping it on the ground below. Nell held her hands up to her face, looking in horror at the whimpering creature on the ground.

'It's too late. She's already gone,' said Nell, a pang of sorrow piercing her heart. 'I'm fine. It wasn't meant to be. Pewksbury can't be that bad.' She didn't believe her own words, and Poco's nods were as convincing as her weak smile. Indy wrapped his tail around her for a moment.

'Let's save this Christmas tree!' she cried through teary eyes. At least defending the tree would be something.

'To battle!' said Poco, sending a pine needle off like a javelin to the next crow that swooped in. 'Take that, sucker!' The crow took a U-turn and headed back into the mist.

Nell unhooked an icicle decoration. It was heavy, so she gripped it with both hands and swished it at the crows that came near. Her whole body tightened with the effort. A group of sheep and other small numins stood nearby, their knees knocking together.

Their eyes flashed white with terror every time a crow swooped in. She hopped down to them and called them over.

'Nibble off a frond of needles,' she said. 'Use it as a shield.' She snapped one off and showed them how to hold it over them. They copied. She looked around her. 'And here. You can use these.' There was a line of candy canes hanging nearby. She raced over and used the sharp end of the icicle decoration to cut the string, unthreaded them and handed them out to the bravest. Others hid further in the tree behind their fronds. 'Have a go.' She swung a candy cane like it was a samurai sword. 'It will give them a bump, enough to put them off.' One sheep's eyes lit up as he made a swooping sound with it.

A crow grabbed another sheep. Nell thumped him on the neck with the icicle. He shrieked, and a bunny bashed him on the beak with his candy cane. The bunny fell onto his back, grinning. The crow retreated to the other side of the square. Nell gave the bunny a high five.

'Good!' said Nell. They were away, swooping their canes, like a fluffy animal army heading forth in battle. 'Keep going.'

Indy stood tall on the tip of the branch, rearing upwards on his hind legs, using his antler and hooves to block the crows from coming in closer. One swooped in fast from the now thick fog. It knocked Indy over onto the branch and snapped off his remaining antler, which fell to the ground far below.

'Aargh!' he cried.

'Indy!' called Nell. Indy stood up.

'I'm fine' he said. 'I'm even now, anyway.' He grinned, returned to his post, and carried on.

The sugar-mice ran about in wild circles. Glacia was nowhere to be seen. A small Christmas stocking nearby bulged and trembled. Glacia's head poked out and called to the sugar mice. She saw a crow pick one of them up and take it over to the railings, and it took it into his beak in one gulp. Nell covered her eyes with her hands. Glacia whimpered, then sank back inside the stocking again.

Ruby joined forces with Ava and the turtledoves. They swooped and pecked at the crows who came near. Another crow swooped in and bit at Ruby's neck. It let out a shrill cry as two turtledoves tied a ribbon around its feet. He retreated and flew haphazardly back toward the railings, landing in a heap on the ground.

The pixies used tinsel to catapult anything they could find at the crows. They sang:

'Come and get us if you dare. We will not be taken to your lair,
If you peck us, we will fight! We don't mind if it takes all night!'

A pine needle arrow shot out of the tree and struck a crow that was heading for Ruby in its breast. It flew away. Another crow headed straight for Nell. She yelled and swiped at it with the icicle, hitting his leg.

'Sorry, but you started it!' He careered down to the ground. Dazed, he shook his whole body, then

130

picked himself up. He flew back, angrier, glaring into Nell's eyes. She glared back. He flew in towards Poco and took him up in his beak, clenching him tight.

'No! Poco!' shouted Nell. Quick as lightening, Nell bounded over to a dangling string of lights, grabbed it, and whipped it up to the flying crow like a lasso. Once it was circled around his neck, she tugged him in as he strained to get free. Poco struggled fiercely, trying to prize open the crow's beak to freedom. The crow pulled at the wire. Nell clambered up the cord and, fuelled by her own determination, she leapt onto the crow's back and closed her arms around his neck. She crawled forwards and pulled at his beak, so it opened enough to release Poco onto the springy branch below.

'Oof!' said Poco, who lay winded on his back and managed to give her a thumbs up. The crow twisted its head to reach Nell who clung on. Trembling, she watched as a pine needle arrow fired from the tree stuck in the feathers of his breast, and another into his wing. Indy, who stretched on his hind legs on the edge of the branch, cut the fairy light line that held the crow with a broken bauble timing it just as he flew above him. The crow crashed down over the edges of the branches to the ground amongst the debris. Nell landed in a heap on the branch next to Poco and Indy. They held each other. Poco pulled a face as he noticed a sheep's tail separated from its body squirming on the branch. He turned away from it and pushed it onto the branch below.

'Yuk!' he said. He fainted. The two pixies bounded over and slapped his face, rather too hard, until he was revived. He sat up, spluttering. They laughed, enjoying it far more than they should.

The battle continued while numins worked together to save the Christmas tree filled with all the hope of their beloved humans. In the darkest moments, more pine needle arrows shot out of the tree and saw off the crows that kept coming. One crow swooped in and landed on the branch from where the arrows shot out. Cawing came from inside of the tree. Nell and Poco stopped to watch. Two more crows gathered there and cawed back. Then three, then five, then ten.

'What are they doing?' asked Indy.

'I don't know,' said Nell. More strange crow calls came from inside the tree as the crows stopped attacking. All the numins stood baffled by the sight. Then, one by one, the crows flew off. They landed on the riverside railings on the side of the square in a row, preening their feathers as if nothing had happened.

CHAPTER 23

MAGICAL MENDING

An ochre sliver of dawn grew on the horizon, glistening in Nell's eyes. The fog had cleared, and a sudden downpour left the giant pine weeping drips of rain onto the ground. The surrounding trees bowed as if in sorrow. The river flowed like a stream of tears. Nell and the other numins now stood not on an inspiring tree of hope and festivity, but among piles of smashed baubles and trashed treasured decorations. Thousands of broken fragments littered the cobbles in the square. Broken lights, ribbons, and tinsel drifted hopelessly in the wind. Many numins were damaged. No one saw the lost sugar-mouse again. A cloak of heartache covered the tree and its residents. It was early on Christmas morning, and the Hope's End Christmas tree was the aftermath of a battle zone. Even the dawn birdsong could not comfort them, nor the scent of baking gingerbread wafting from the boat. The golden violin drifted in, doing its best to play a hopeful tune. The injured gathered on the lower branches to rest.

'Oh, dear.' Otto the nutcracker sniffed as he sat down. He held up a piece of the broken sprout in his hands. 'Let us sit around and tell sad stories.' Nell put her hand on his shoulder.

'No,' she said. 'Let us get to work and clear up this mess!'

'Oh, yes, that's a much better idea. Let's do that. Forget mine.' He stood up and wiped away his tears. 'Let's go.'

Nell and Poco inspected the damage. Ava, Ruby, and the turtledoves restrung the lights, looping garlands and tinsel across the branches using their beaks. Some numins rehung baubles and decorations that were still intact. Kevin, Anka, and Mick the post box made a ladder from the twinkling lights that reached to the ground to fetch fallen treasures. The Indian elephant chanted softly, his hands resting on his knees. Nell, Indy, Poco and many others helped put things back.

'I suppose I had better get to work now,' sighed Ziggy the sloth, who had slept through the whole thing. She shuffled slowly along to reach the injured and broken. When she got into position, she scratched her nose, yawned, and took the piece of broken Sprout from the sniffing Otto. Nell and Poco moved closer.

'Watch me everyone.' Ziggy held the fragment

close to her belly, closed her eyes and sang:

'Back to how you're meant to be!
Whole again in time for tea
What's done undone, become like new
Cracks gone, breaks healed,
by the numin healing few'

The fragment flashed. Shattered pieces of sprout zoomed from across the branches to re-join to the first. The other numins ducked out of the way. Nell gaped as bright light fizzed over the broken edges, which fused together like an automatic jigsaw puzzle. Ziggy yawned again, handing Sprout to Otto, as if it was the easiest thing in the world. Otto dropped to his knees and held her up, crying tears of joy.

'Sprout!' he said. She shook herself, then bounced out of Otto's hands and staggered around like she was drunk. She beamed at everyone and jumped about.

'I'm alive! Alive!' she said. 'Sproutball, anyone?'

'Blinking baubles, Ziggy!' said Nell, her eyes sparkling. 'That's amazing!' She gazed at her, resting her hand against her cheek. Ruby flew over and showered Ziggy in excited gold sparks. 'Let's pass everything to Ziggy!' said Nell.

'Wow!' said Poco. 'Can I have your address? It won't matter if I fall now!' Indy chuckled. Numins from all over brought broken pieces to Ziggy to mend.

'Some of you can do it, too. Everyone may as well try, and I wouldn't mind a nap soon. Grab a piece and listen carefully.'

The numins each picked a broken fragment and listened, Nell held a fractured chunk of what looked like a blue bottle she had seen earlier. Poco clutched something black and woolly.

'Hold a fragment in your middle, nice and tight,' said Ziggy. 'Now, remember your awakening moment. Think hard now. Feel the glow inside?' They all nodded. 'When you are ready, say the rhyme. With me.' They all joined in:

'Back to how you're meant to be,
whole again in time for tea,
What's done undone, become like new,
Cracks gone; breaks healed!
by the numin healing few'

Nell's blue bottle stayed as it was, so she handed it to the pom-pom snowman, who held it close to his tummy, and the broken pieces flew in and re-joined in a zip of light. He beamed and held the bottle up high, as good as new. A turtle dove picked it up in his beak and carried it back to where it came from.

'Brilliant!' said Nell, clapping him on the back.

The angry Santa tried with a fractured piece of dark pink glass. He was so cross that it didn't work that he threw it down at Ziggy's feet. A bunny picked it up and had a go, his sister held a similar section. The pieces glowed bright white and zipped together like magnets, taking the bunnies with them, bumping their heads. More shards whizzed towards them from every direction. They fell about giggling and the beetroot decoration hopped out of their paws and bobbed around with Sprout.

Poco held his piece close to him. Nothing happened, so he handed it to Ziggy. Ziggy picked it up between thumb and forefinger and nestled it in her belly and said the rhyme. The sheep that had fallen to the ground whizzed up and joined its tail. Poco covered his mouth in disgust and fainted again. They all clapped as the sheep ran around in circles, trying to see his tail.

Nell and the other numins formed a chain, passing the broken fragments along to those with the healing skill, humming as they worked. The glass dragonfly numin flitted over them, whispering sounds of encouragement to them. Others place the mended decorations back around the tree as they returned to their bases.

'Emma could use this kind of help for tidying her room,' said Nell, her smile fading as she remembered she may not see her ever again.

Opus and the choir arrived in a line, still tied together.

'Well, what have we missed?'

'Opus!' said Nell, bounding over and squeezing him in a tight hug. 'What are you doing here?'

'We wanted to help. I found my courage, ha!' Nell wouldn't let go. 'We got stuck in traffic, though, that hot-air balloon is so unreliable.' He patted her back, then pulled away and pointed to a scratch on his head. 'I got caught by a falling shard of glass. My first injury in centuries! Lovely to see you, dear Nell.' He smiled knowingly and squeezed her hand.

'I didn't make it,' she said, fighting back tears.

'All we can ever do is our best!' he said. 'Something will turn up, you'll see.' He spoke softly and gave her another squeeze. A small smile crept into the corner of her lip. 'Now, where is our missing member?' Poco jumped over, flapping his arms in all directions as he explained everything to them.

'Poco, I should have believed in you. I am sorry. Sometimes there are greater things to deal with than staying glossy, eh?'

'Apology accepted, old man.' Poco slapped him on the back. 'Does that mean I can take flying lessons now?' Opus covered his face with his palm.

The choir stood in an arc and sang songs about hope and faith, accompanied by the violin. When Opus saw what Ziggy was doing, he hurried over.

'Remarkable!' He bowed low. 'Do you work with 15th century cherry wood?' he asked, pointing to his scratch.

Ziggy opened her eyes and grabbed Opus pulling his head close to her tummy.

'Oh well, really! I meant that—' Before he could finish, Opus's scratch disappeared in a flash of light. He patted where the scratch had been. 'Oh, wonderful workmanship. You will always be welcome at Hawthorn House.' He bowed, the redness of his cheeks melting away.

'Your turn.' Nell smiled to Indy, nodding at his antlerless head, and nudging him towards the snowman. He bowed his head into the snowman's woolly tummy and waited. In a flash, his antler flew up between the branches and re-joined his head with a twang. He rubbed it.

'A miracle! Thank you.' He gave the snowman a low bow too, who bounced up and down. Everyone cheered. Glacia approached Ziggy. The two remaining sugar-mice scuttled around her.

'What about my mouse?' She dabbed at her tears with her tutu.

Ziggy shook her head. 'I am sorry.' Nell, Poco and the numins nearby stood holding each other's hands, heads bowed. Glacia wept.

The turtledoves lifted a large gold paper mâché star in their beaks to the top of the tree and placed it where the angel had been. The numins worked at mending and replacing the treasures until the warm light of Christmas morning reached the square. They restored the tree to its former glory. The trees' branches lifted and dipped in the wind, as if breathing a sigh of relief.

As they admired their work, and Nell wondered what on earth she was going to do now, the grubby figure Nell had saved swung in on a red cord and jumped into the clearing. He wandered over to Ziggy, holding his injured side, his satchel bursting with long pine needle arrows.

She waved to him. She remembered the pine arrows coming from the tree when she first arrived, and during the battle. Her mind whirred. He waved back.

'Glad you're free!' he said. Her eyes widened. How did he know? He waved to Ruby, who swooped around him in a circle, sparking red sparks all over him.

'Who is that?' asked Indy.

'He's the snatcher.' Indy looked at her. 'It's complicated.' She shrugged.

Opus and Poco and all the other singers looked over at the stranger. The choir stopped singing. He lifted his satchel up for Ziggy to work on his injured side. A bright flash of light shone out from it as the sloth did her work. The injury healed. Dirt and grime fell away revealing bright red clothes.

Nell, Opus and Poco's mouths fell open, as they all at once realised who it was. Nell's heart thumped.

'It's Red!' shouted Poco, bounding over to him. 'Red's back!'

CHAPTER 24

SAVING HOPE'S END

'Red!' Poco jumped into his arms.

'Hello little fella!' Red grinned. 'Good to see you again!' He hugged him tight. 'So, you are here on the tree too, are you?' he said.

Opus and the others crowded around and took it in turns to hug him, while Ruby flitted above him, firing red sparks.

'You're alive!' said Opus through teary eyes. He shook both his hands in his. 'I thought we would find you again, dear Red!'

'I missed you lot. I am alive thanks to this one.' He nodded to Nell and held out his hand to her. She shook it.

'So, you're Red?' Her eyes lit up. 'And it was you

who fired the arrows? You who found the key and sent Ruby to me in Vaspar's cage?'

'It was a team effort,' he said, smiling at Ava who rested on a branch above them. Ava smiled and bowed to him, then to Nell. Ruby covered him in beaky kisses.

'Hey!' he said, blushing.

'Thank you all, for freeing me,' said Nell, the warmth of new friends twinkling through her once more. Red reached in his satchel and threw Opus's staff to him.

'Oh, you found it, thank goodness!' said Nell.

'Catch!' Opus caught it and gazed at it lovingly in his hands and clutched it to his heart.

'Red, enlighten us. Where have you been? How did you get this?' He waved his staff in the air. 'How do you know our Nell, and–' He looked him up and down. 'Why on earth were you so dirty? Were there no baths where you've been?' Red laughed.

'Charming as ever, Opus!' he said. 'It is a long story. How is Hawthorn House?'

Nell looked from Opus to Red. She was about to speak when a strange tugging sensation pulled inside her head. She fell onto the branch and held her head in her hands.

'Oooh!' she said, gripping her head.

Red, Indy, Poco and the others gathered around her. A powerful energy filled her like an earthquake from within. She held on to Poco and Red, who steadied her.

'What's the matter, Nell?' asked Poco.

'What is it?' said Opus, holding Poco and

142

Melody's hands a little too tight.

'My head feels strange! I think this is it. It is – the end! I'm finally dying. Emma doesn't need me, because I left, or that I failed my mission or whatever. I don't know. Anyway, I am dying, and I deserve it. I was a terrible numin, let's face it. Totally useless. Goodbyeeee–' She collapsed in a dramatic heap. The numins looked at each other, as Ruby sprayed white sparks everywhere. Nell lay still, waiting for death. With her little heart drumming away as before, and the starlight swirling brighter than ever and very much still alive, she opened one eye a crack. Her friends huddled around her, peering in with puzzled faces.

'Are you sure Nell, you seemed alright just now,' said Opus. 'It's unusual to die all of a sudden like that. And such a new numin too. Could it be something else? Perhaps you are not, in fact, dead?' He looked at the others, then back to Nell. 'What are you feeling?'

'Wait, I see something,' she said. Still clutching her head, she sat up. A vision of another place curled into her mind.

'What Nell? What can you see?' asked Poco, barging forwards.

'Something strange is happening to me.' Her friends circled around her. Her ears burned hot.

'Tell us!' said Opus.

'I see a door with wooden panels, and, oh, it's opening. There is a large desk, drawers on either side and–' Ava and Opus looked at each other. 'There is a man, a wide man. Oh, it is Mr Slug, Mr Tribulus, looking out of the window at the green sky. He is sitting on a chair with his head in his hands. There are papers on the desk, and a computer. This happened before! I had a dream about Emma and her mother when I was in the birdcage, it felt like this.' Opus leaned in closer and dropped his voice low and clear.

'Nell, when you were with that Vaspar, is there any way he might have, well, did he do anything–odd?'

'Oh, I forgot! So much has been happening, there hasn't been any time. Yes, he did something strange. After Glacia took Poco away, he put me in a birdcage.' They all glared at Glacia.

'I'm sorry about that.' Glacia looked down at her feet.

'He had this round thing. He held it up to my eyes, and it flashed. It felt strange, but it only lasted a second.'

'The Orb of Soul Essence,' said Ava. 'It has been safe for centuries, but it recently went missing.' She lowered her eyes. Opus nodded and tapped his chin, now pacing around Nell.

'Yes, I remember it, for translocating souls,' he said.

'The what?' Nell's eyes widened. 'For what?' Ava and Opus looked at each other.

'The light from the sunset shifts a soul fragment through the orb from one to another,' said Ava. 'To restore life.'

'We think Vaspar took a piece of your soul, Nell,' said Opus.

'He *what*?' Her hands flew onto her hips.

'Wow, that is just so creepy,' said Poco, shivering.

'You don't say?' Nell flapped her arms out. 'It was my soul!'

'Well, we are here now,' said Opus. 'You have a soul-connection with Vaspar. You and he are bonded by souls. And it seems that Vaspar is Mr Tribulus's numin.'

'Oh, well, this is just flipping fantastic! That's all I need! Fail Emma completely and now an evil fake king and a greedy slug attached to my soul. Ger-eat.' She crossed her arms.

'Woah!' said Poco, rubbing his hands together.

'Nell,' said Opus. 'You are looking through Vaspar. This is happening right now for a reason. This may be a chance to change something. To change Mr Tribulus. To change everything!' He nodded and smiled. 'It takes a powerful numin to do this, Nell, whatever is about to happen. And we believe in you!' He placed his little hand on her shoulder. 'So, what can you see?'

'Huh?' Nell stared at him. She focused. The centre of her vision was like a screen. She saw the desk Vaspar could see. Vaspar ran over to Tribulus, climbed up the chair leg and Tribulus's back, and looked down at the desk from his shoulder.

'Okay. Vaspar is with Mr Tribulus. He is on his shoulder, judging by the massive hairy earlobe. There is a paper with something about Pewksbury written on it on the desk. It's a report.' Her stomach clenched. 'No, no, this is too weird and creepy. I don't want to bond with them, I–'

'Stay strong, Nell,' said Poco, placing his hand on her other shoulder, barely able to contain his excitement. They all stared at her and waited.

'Ok, I just don't want to connect with them, like, forever.' She braced herself.

'You won't. Just keep a tight hold of your own life force inside, never lose yourself! Now, what is this report?' said Opus. They all leaned in towards Nell, their arms, and wings around each other.

'It's a report about Pewksbury,' she said. 'About a factory.' Her voice strained. She went quiet as she read.

'Well, come on, what does it say?' said Poco, hopping from foot to foot.

'Oh!' She put her hands to her ashen face and gulped. 'It says that the factory, his factory in Pewksbury, it is spewing toxic chemicals into the air. It is not a disease, it's him and his stupid poisonous factory! It says that's why the sky is weird and green!' Anger burned through her. 'That's why Emma's dad is ill, and all the others. It was Tribulus all along! And I think that's the factory where Emma's mother has gone to work!' The friends looked at each other, lost for words. Ava flapped her wings and Ruby's beak let out a green fireball.

'He totally lost the plot!' said Poco, ducking out of the way, then stroking Ruby's chest to soothe her.

'Oh, my goodness,' said Opus. He pulled Poco and Melody towards him and stared at Nell.

'That all makes sense now,' said Indy, looking out to the town with its odd green clouds floating above.

'The sickness must have started as soon as they

opened that factory,' said Opus. 'We are downwind from there.'

'That must have been when all those fish died. Did you hear about that?' said Red, shaking his head.

'Gosh, Tribulus was a rotter!' said Opus.

'Was?' asked Nell, her face still pale.

'Yes, Was. No wonder that powerful connection between you formed. Because you can stop it, Nell. And you must. Right now.' Her insides clenched tightly.

'Me?' She held her hand to her chest and gaped at him.

'Vaspar is there. Talk to him.' Opus leaned in. 'Use your link to make him a better numin and stop Mr Tribulus. You can make him do the right thing. He will have your goodwill in his soul, and he won't be able to ignore it.' The group glanced at each other. Opus held his arms out and smiled encouragingly. 'Kindness is your superpower, Nell! Ha! Now is the time to talk.'

'You can do it, Nell,' said Indy, nudging her with his snout. 'You can save the town.'

'Didn't I say?' said Poco. 'Find his heart, I said! I did, didn't I?' He grinned, shaking his own hand in congratulations.

'Yeah, you were a great help with that, Poco.' She felt a little queasy. 'How do I talk to him?'

'Use your mind. Concentrate on your awakening, the starlight feeling, and what matters most and, well, talk!' Opus smiled. 'I must say, this Vaspar got more than he bargained for when he stole your soul, Nell! Ha!' He nudged Poco and Red. 'Eh? And an absolutely massive mission in your first few days of numinhood! What an awakening!' He quivered. Seeing Nell's furrowed brow, he looked at her tenderly and put his hand on hers. 'Have faith in yourself!'

'You can do it,' said Poco. She nodded gently to them, her heart anchored with trust in her friends, and closed her eyes. She remembered awakening in Emma's cosy red pocket, looking at the angel. The tingling as Emma had made the wish. The starlight swirling inside. Her passion to make the wish come true. The feeling grew strong. She tingled again, like popping candy fizzing in her body. Perhaps Emma's wish could still come true.

'Vaspar!' she said. He looked all around him to see where the voice was coming from. 'Vaspar it's Nell! Our souls are linked.'

'Blinking baubles! Nell, Sweet Nell!' said Vaspar. 'You're in my head now? Well, this day is getting better by the minute! And I'm sorry! I did it! I am so sorry! For everything. For taking your soul, for putting you in the birdcage. For asking my beetles to hurt your friends, that white bird and the bizarre fire robin thingy, whatever it is, when they went to look for you. And the grubby fellow who is always in the way. But I've changed. I have come back to life. Your soul has changed me, Nell! I see how you see things and want to help! This beautiful world, these wonderful humans! I mean, sure, they get a lot wrong and are often in such a muddle. Embarrassing, really! And boy, some eye-watering mistakes! But they are our beloved humans! Walking miracles, the lot of them. I want to help them too! And Nell, I have something important to tell you!'

'Vaspar, I saw that paper on the table. Mr Tribulus owns that factory, and it's making everyone ill. The fumes are drifting over Hope's End from Pewksbury because we are downwind. It is his fault that the town has gone to ruin! We have to stop him.' She let a heavy breath out and waited.

'Oh, he is such a twit isn't he! No wonder I was half dead and hopeless! Poisoning the town to make more money. You couldn't make it up!'

'Vaspar, you must tell him to stop,' said Nell. 'Try a dream whisper. Tell him to find his heart, remember all the people whose lives he is ruining. Tell him to do the right thing. To close the factory.'

'Yes, alright, and then you have to know what else I have been doing!'

'There is no time, Vaspar, people are ill. The town is desperate. Focus! We can stop it! Do it now!' she said, her eyes wide open. Her friends leaned in and nodded encouragingly. In her vision, Vaspar whispered to Mr Tribulus, Nell couldn't hear what, but it sounded gentle and kind. Mr Tribulus paused for a long while. Then he wailed and sobbed into his hands.

'Oh, what a terrible mess!' he said. He clutched his head in his hands. 'It's all my fault. Everything is my fault!'

'Tell him to pick up the phone and stop it, Vaspar! Close that blinking factory down!' Nell could not hear Vaspar's words. Sitting up straight she saw Mr Tribulus place his trembling hand on the phone. At that moment, he disappeared.

'There is something else, Nell, I–' The image and sound faded away and Vaspar and Mr Tribulus were gone.

'Vaspar, wait!' She looked up at her friends circled around her. 'He's gone.'

'Oh, well done Nell! That's what the fellowship is about, ha!' Opus leaned towards her and patted her shoulder. 'Very well done indeed.' Her friends clapped and patted each other, and her, on the back. 'I suspect that your soul-bond channel broke because the task is complete! Vaspar is a full numin again, with a heart! He doesn't need you anymore, nor does Tribulus as he found his heart too. We shall have to see, but I believe you have done all you can.' They all cheered and hugged each other. All except Nell.

'Done?' Tears welled in her eyes. 'I mean, that's all great and everything, but what about Emma? The link is gone. She's gone. That was my chance to get her back. Do I just forget about her? Do I try to find her in Pewksbury? I don't even know where it is!'

CHAPTER 25

THE CROWS

Nell wiped her tears on her sleeve. Red sidled over to her, his hands in his pockets. He gave her a nervous smile.

'I am sorry if this is a bad time,' he said, shifting around, 'but I have to tell you about the crows. It's kind of urgent.'

'Oh, yes, I forgot. Do you know why they attacked and stopped so suddenly? It was odd.' The crows still rested on the park railings as if nothing had happened. Nell was glad of a distraction from the emptiness that stretched inside her. She straightened up. The numins looked from Red to the crows and back again. 'Well?'

'Before Christmas, when the humans set up the Christmas tree, and you all turned up.' Red smiled at Opus, Poco and the choir. 'I didn't know you would be here too. I thought you were way too old and special. Or I would have come to find you straight away!' The choir crowded around and hugged him again.

'Less of the old, please!' said Opus with a smile. Red grinned.

'Anyway, when I told the crows that town was taking over their tree, they were so angry. Where would they roost? This year was terrible for them too. No food. They were hungry and thin. They resented you for taking their home. The only two things they fear are man and starvation. Then, on that first day, some people shooed them aside. They didn't want them close, covering the tree with bird poo and scaring small children, ruining the atmosphere, or whatever it was. Someone even talked about giving them bird killer. Crows are intelligent, they understood. It was too much.' Glacia looked up to the sky, avoiding their gazes. Nell remembered Glacia has an owner, too, probably not a nice one, and felt sorry for her.

'Not exactly a symbol of hope and inspiration the town needed. Since then, the crows have been watching you and getting more and more angry since you took over their tree.'

'I can't say I didn't notice.' Nell huffed and folded her arms looking over to them preening their feathers. The numins muttered crow-related opinions to each other.

'We came over after living on the other side of the river after they ran out of food. This was their new roost. They are intelligent, though not always kind. Especially if they are hungry. So, they attacked. I tried to stop them. They want to ruin the tree, make the whole idea a failure and Hope's End to never to do this again. Well, I'm numin too. I love humans and I don't want that. The crows took me, but they have been good to me since then. Without them I'd have been lost, or worse.'

'Oh, dear Red, what a life!' said Opus, wiping away tears.

'The crows kept me going. But this attack was a step too far. I knew the humans would be back here today for Christmas Day. I had to stop the attack. That's why I came up with a plan.' He smiled.

'Oh, good. I was hoping there would be a plan. What, Red?' Nell asked, her eyes a little brighter.

'Yes, what plan?' said Poco, clasping his hands together. They all chimed in and looked at him, waiting. Red took a long breath.

'They are hungry. There are loads of edible decorations on the tree, right? Iced biscuits, chocolate coins, clove oranges, apple stars, nut garlands, cranberry hearts,' he said, looking around. Poco still had his chocolate coin shield and waved it about. 'There's enough here for a crow feast. They are afraid of shiny objects, and the edible decorations are in disguise. It didn't occur to them to look for food here. So, I told them you would bring all the edible decorations to the front, and they agreed they would stop the attack.'

'Great idea. When?' asked Nell, clapping her hands. The numins rippled with excitement.

'At dawn,' he said.

'But its dawn now,' said Nell, her heart thumping. He grinned.

'I said it was urgent.' They all glanced at each other, at the crows, then around the tree. Dotted everywhere hung iced biscuits, hazelnut hearts, and dried apple stars. There were clove oranges and bunches of sugared almonds. Gingerbread shapes tied in red ribbons. Chocolate coins and candy canes, dried cranberry hearts, and so many more. Poco started stretching his legs.

'Well, what are we waiting for!' said Nell. Her fierce heart thumped in her chest. 'We know we make a wonderful team!' She opened her arms, and each looked around them at the magnificent, restored tree. Wonder filled their hearts. The Christmas tree shimmered with even more beauty and dazzle than before. 'We can work together!' They clapped.

'Yes!' they cried, and 'beautiful!' and 'let's go!' They moved off to collect the food.

Indy trotted towards a garland of dried orange slices covered in gold sugar dust.

'Not too much chocolate,' said Nell.

'No, it makes them burp,' said Red. Poco sniggered as he unhooked a gingerbread star. The pixies turned up and let out several fake burps, each one louder than the one before.

'Those who can fly can collect from the farthest parts. The rest of us can form teams and go foraging.

We have no time to lose. The sun is coming up, so the humans will be here for their Christmas gathering soon.'

Nell was glad she could make herself useful again, even if she had failed Emma. At least Emma's father may get well again now. That would make her happy. She sighed. The numins formed groups heading in different directions to gather the edible ornaments. 'Oh, Merry Christmas everyone!' said Nell. Red held out his hand and Nell shook it.

'Merry Christmas!' They each stopped for a moment to shake hands, hug, pat each other's backs, and wave across the branches to their new friends. The words 'Merry Christmas!' spread around the tree like a festive wave. As they focussed on gathering, nobody noticed a small figure appear in the gap in the yew hedge in the far corner of the square. He ran out of the gloom toward the tree, waving his arms about in the new light of Christmas morning.

CHAPTER 26

CHRISTMAS BREAKFAST

Nell tucked walnuts under her arms, their silver ribbons trailing behind as she went in search of Otto, to see if he could crack them with his fearsome nut-cracking mouth. Indy stacked iced biscuits and headed to the front with Poco. The rest of the choir passed a string of hazelnuts along. Glacia followed behind with a dried cranberry heart, admiring the red jewel berries, her remaining sugar mice at her heels. The mice skewered apple stars and orange slices onto their ski poles, batting away the pixies who were trying to bite chunks out of them. Ruby held her breath so as not to burn a bag of sugared almonds she carried in her beak. The pompom snowman staggered under the weight of a stack of chocolate coins balanced on his head. The geese loaded cinnamon sticks across the sausage dogs' backs. The numins gathered at the front of the tree with the offerings. Otto set to work, cracking the nuts that Nell and others brought to him to open. It might have been impressive, though he dribbled pieces of nutshell down through the branches. It was disgusting. Nell and Glacia had to look away. The pixies did an impression, dribbling all over the place and cackling. The crows watched and waited.

The sun hung low above the horizon, dripping her soft amber light over the decorations. The numins laid the food on the branches at the front of the tree. Red whistled the crows over. Nell placed her hands on her hips and watched as they swooped in to collect it. They took the food in their beaks and wolfed it down. Ava and Ruby, the turtledoves and more winged numins, collected up fallen debris from the ground. They carried leftover rubbish and wrappers and discarded ribbon pieces to the litter bins. Glacia threw cranberries out to the crows, which they caught in mid-air. She smiled at Nell and glided over to her.

'Nell, sorry for being horrible to you. It is no excuse, but I was jealous.' She sighed. 'My owners, the Smythes only love how I look. And now, not even that. They put me in a box for years until this week. Once, I was on the top of our tree, but they found a horrible, jewelled star to replace me. Instead of trying to make things better by being a great numin, I became bitter.' Poco wandered over to them with his hands in his pockets. 'I just hated having to look perfect all the time!' she continued. Nell nodded. 'I would much rather be normal like all of you, thinking about more important things, not always trying to look pristine and perfect! I hate it!' Poco, still covered in smudges, shrugged. He wiped his grubby hand down her dress leaving a grimy smear.

'You're welcome,' he said, and wandered on, his hands back in his pockets. Glacia looked down at her grubby dress and blinked. Nell stared at the mess, and they both folded over in laughter.

'Can you forgive me?' She looked down at her feet. Nell placed her hand on Glacia's arm.

'I am sorry about your family.' She smiled. 'I was lucky with Emma.' Her heart tightened. Would she ever see her again?

'And now Vaspar has disappeared.' said Glacia. 'Perhaps the crows took him too,' she said, biting her nail. 'I know he is horrid, but he is my friend.'

'I am sure he will be back,' said Nell.

After a time, the tree was bare of the edibles. The square was clear once more. A line of rounder, happier crows fluffed themselves up along the riverside railings for a morning nap. Nell waved at them, and a few flapped their wings back at her. They snoozed just as you might after stuffing in a huge Christmas dinner.

Numins across the tree chatted, exchanging names and addresses, tips, and skills. They told each other about magical objects they had heard of that were lost, like the orb, and shared ideas about what on earth that blue bottle was. Rumours of treasures for time-travel, invisibility, or portals to other places spread. Mick and Kevin went with Anka, the llama and the geese to find them on the tree, and more followed. The mice, sausage dogs and vegetables went too, with the dragonfly fluttering above, the cat strolling behind.

The numins went back to their original places as the humans began to arrive in the square. Nell and the others swung on the tinsel and lights where they could, travelling back to base. The choir on Indy and Ava's backs, Poco on Red's shoulders.

The church bells began to ring out. Nell's chest swelled with pride. When they arrived, Nell let out a long breath as they settled onto their branch.

The choir sang Winter Wonderland into the stillness of Christmas morning. Plump snowflakes fell, and soon the sky was dizzy with them. Nell turned her face up and the cool flakes peppered her face. She wondered if it was snowing in Pewksbury. She hoped Emma would be happy, whatever happened next. She had friends now and was grateful for them.

People gathered by the Christmas tree to admire it and listen to the human choir who had arrived and were singing Christmas carols. Children tried to catch the snowflakes in their mouths, and the adults chatted. A man roasted chestnuts, and people ate them with hot chocolate and mulled wine, warming their gloved hands on the cups. Some gathered around his stove and toasted marshmallows over the flame for breakfast. Church goers made their way to the church behind.

Nell gazed longingly at the families having fun. A pang of envy pierced her heart. At least the town was going to get back to normal. She looked around the tree at the numins dotted around. Friends. A soft wind blew from the river, loaded with the promise of more snow. Wind swept under the branches and the tree, which rose and fell, as if to let out a great, long sigh.

*

'Pssst.' A small figure arrived underneath the tree where Nell and the others sat listening to the choir. 'Help me up!' said Vaspar, with a big smile on his face. Eight little wooden faces and Nell peered down at him.

'What do you want?' said Opus, looking over and frowning. Vaspar was still a stranger to him.

'I want to come up!' Ruby flew over and blew black and white sparks above him. Nell and the others peered down. 'Dear Nell! I have to tell you what happened!' he said. Ava, who rested on a nearby branch, flew to join them.

'You look different, Vaspar,' said Indy. His face was now smooth and bright, the cracks and nobbles had gone, and his eyes shone as warm and bright as the others. His coat was now a smooth, warm grey with gold edges. He waved at them.

'Oh, I missed you, fellow numins!'

After a lot of winching and pulling, Vaspar was

back on the tree, hugging everyone warmly.

'That's better!' he said, dusting himself off.

'Vaspar!' Glacia slid down a long cord of crystal beads to him. They hugged.

'Well, Vaspar, are you going to tell us what happened?' asked Nell, her hands on her hips. 'Did it really work?'

CHAPTER 27

CHESTNUTS IN RIVERSIDE SQUARE

'Attention friends!' Vaspar raised his arms in the air. 'In case you didn't know, Nell is innocent!' Vaspar turned to her and bowed so low that his nose touched his knees. Nell's cheeks burned pink. 'And I am sorry. Please forgive me for being dreadful to you, and for trying to break from the humans. Nell, Indy, and Ava are all correct. The humans need us, and we need them! Without them we have no meaning, no life even. We must strengthen our bonds, not take them away. Just like Nell said!' He lifted her arm and waved it about. Nell smiled awkwardly. How embarrassing. 'I have been a fool. Forgive me.' He turned to Red. 'I am sorry that I pushed you off that branch when you discovered my secret. And that I set my rather frightening friends on you.' Red shrugged.

'As long as you don't do it again!' he said. Vaspar hung his head and nodded. Ruby folded her wings and scowled.

'Oh, and you, I am sorry for your little accident with your wing the other morning when I came back for Nell.' He turned to Nell. 'You have a loyal friend there! I'm glad you escaped. I guess I wasn't as clever as I thought!'

'What happened, Vaspar?' she asked.

'I wasn't a good numin, it's true. My owners, I am afraid, were bad people. Tribulus only ever liked money. I failed him. I didn't make him a better human, I only let him make me a worse numin. Because of that, I was dying. I wanted to live and didn't care about anything else. I was greedy for life! Instead of helping my humans live with love and hope in their lives, which might have saved me anyway, I just wanted to save myself.' He hung his head. 'When I saw Nell and her brand-new soul practically shining, I am afraid it tempted me, yes. I used this.' He took the orb from his pocket and held it up. The numins moved closer and peered at it. Some gasped. Misty grey swirled inside like a tornado in slow motion.

'Wooah!' said Poco.

'This is the Orb of Soul Essence. I found it when—'

'You found it in the bookshop when Mr Tribulus made Bob close it and clear out,' said Ava. Her eyes narrowed. She flapped her wings, her bell sounding, and sending nearby baubles swinging. She turned to the others. 'Mr Tribulus raised the rent while the town was in crisis. So, Bob had to close the shop, after twenty years there.' Ava glared at Vaspar. 'And that is our orb. It is one of the most precious and ancient numin objects known,' she spat, her bell ringing loud. 'Although Bob doesn't know what it is. I am afraid I was trying so hard to find a solution for him and the bookshop that I failed to protect it.'

'Yes, Ava. I found it there that day; I couldn't believe my luck! I heard about it long ago. It was tucked inside a book in the bookshop. All I needed was to find a new numin soul.' He looked at Nell.

'I was its guardian. I let it fall into the wrong hands.' Ava's voice wavered. Indy nudged her with his antler and smiled at her.

'It wasn't your fault,' he said.

'I should have been more careful. I will take it,' said Ava. 'Could someone help?' Red handed her a little Christmas stocking, and they dropped the orb inside for safekeeping.

'Anyway, Nell, I found you, and your soul,' said Vaspar.

'I still can't believe it. I mean, you took my soul?' Frowning, she put her hand on her hip.

'Not all of your soul. But still, it was wrong. It was what I needed to stay alive. It's no excuse, I know. Now I am a different numin, thanks to you. Happier. I feel, well, love.' He grabbed Nell and Glacia and hugged them tight. Nell cringed, then broke into a smile. 'I promise I will use my life more wisely this time around.'

'You had better,' said Nell, giving him a sharp

look.

'When you took Nell's soul, you took on her qualities too,' said Ava. 'A good thing too.' She smiled warmly at Nell. 'It won't last, Vaspar. You must find another way to keep your soul alive from now on. By helping others as they help you. It is the only way. You can't just go around taking peoples souls without asking!' Ava turned to Nell. 'A new soul like yours will not be affected, Nell. That is why they are special.'

'Phew! Thank you!' she let out a puff of air.

'So, did it really work?' asked Nell. 'Did Tribulus do something? Is the town safe now?'

'Yes Nell.' Vaspar stood up again and sighed. He looked out towards the gap in the yew hedge. 'Tribulus closed the factory. Thanks to you! Well done, Nell!' Spots of colour appeared on her cheeks again. Everyone clapped. 'He has told the mayor and word is spreading. The hospitals have been told the cause, so they can cure the sick. Nell—' he said, 'your soul started its work on me before our connection in the office. While you were still in the birdcage. Your mission to make Emma's wish come true took me over then.' Nell stared at him and leaned closer, fidgeting with her plaits.

'What do you mean?' she said.

'Christmas Eve was the strangest day. I was all smiles and joy after I took on your soul. I had a vision of a girl, and I ran straight home, I couldn't help it!'

'And?' Nell clasped her hands together.

'I had no idea what I was doing! Because it was

Emma's wish, your mission, that was driving me. The wish came with the piece of your soul I took. All I knew was that I had to do everything in my power to get Tribulus to stop Emma and her mother from leaving.'

'So, wishes on new numins are so strong they can be passed on. Fascinating,' said Opus, stroking his chin. Nell didn't take her eyes off Vaspar.

'Well?' she said.

'I went home when you were in the birdcage. I jumped in through my letterbox, found Tribulus in his study, and hopped into his pocket. Like I did when he was a boy, and that was last century! Inside the pocket, next to an old pork pie wrapper, a used tissue, and a fifty-pound note, I saw Emma's mother's card, with her phone number and address.'

'He put it his pocket at the square that day,' said Nell.

'I had a good feeling like starlight inside, and I snuck the card out onto the table in front of him. He didn't notice at first. Humans never notice what we do, do they? They are so caught up in their human world!' A chuckle of agreement rippled through them. 'Tribulus was adding up the money he had saved by closing the bookshop and other businesses, and by increasing Emma's mother's rent. There were dozens more on the list, too. What a way to spend Christmas Eve! Yes, well, anyway, he was so interested in counting his money that he didn't notice me climb onto his shoulder. So, I gave him a kiss!'

'Ew,' said Poco, who pretended to be sick. The

pixies laughed. They were back swinging on their loop of tinsel and joined in, folding themselves over and making the most disgusting sounds.

'I know. And I didn't mind at all. I was full of love! I told him he was a kind and thoughtful man deep down. I told him he could be fun, and clever. I said he was handsome too, before he behaved in such an ugly way. I told him he was loved, just as he was. Because I felt it! Tribulus blinked and put his hand to his heart. I said he had nothing to prove, that he didn't need to be so rich. I said that it wasn't too late. I was filled with compassion, and I think I passed it on! Then, I whispered Emma's wish to him. Tribulus picked up the business card and looked at it. He stared up at an old black-and-white picture on the wall of his own mother, who died long ago. She was smiling and wore a battered old hat. Next to her stood a little boy with no shoes on and rather dirty feet. It was him! That was just before I came into their house. Anyway, Mr Tribulus cried. Big, fat tears rolled down his face. I slid back into his pocket as he was about to get up. It takes some planning because he's rather heavy. Funnily enough, he then slipped his hand in his pocket and pulled me out.

'"Oh, it's you!" he said. "How did you get in there?" In the old days he would have shouted and thrown me across the room.' The numins gasped. 'But he didn't. He stroked my cheek and said, "my old friend!" He smiled at me and kissed me on the head! Then he stood up and put me in his pocket with the card.

'He hurried out of the door and along the street

to the other side of town. He knocked on a front door with a bumblebee knocker, puffing and panting. A woman opened it. She had dark circles under her eyes and a black bin bag in her hand, and a child with her. As soon as she saw Mr Tribulus, the girl crossed her arms and scowled. I thought I heard her say "slug."' Nell's heart skipped a beat. She moved her hands to her face, her eyes fixed on Vaspar. 'He explained to the woman that, of course, she could delay paying the rent until she was ready, and that he was sorry. The rent price wasn't going up, but down. He said it had been a mistake. A m-m-mistake. He said that with difficulty.' Nell could barely contain the mix of emotion buzzing inside.

'And?' she said.

'Then the woman leapt forward and gave him a massive hug! I don't think anyone has done that for a long time! She said to her daughter, "Emma, isn't that wonderful!" The girl ran around, then did some sort of robot dance. So, my dear–' Vaspar turned and smiled at Nell, whose eyes were full of tears as she gazed out to the humans bustling on the cobbles.

'They stayed,' she whispered. Emma and her mother were standing in the square eating chestnuts, admiring the magnificent Hope's End Christmas tree.

CHAPTER 28

CHRISTMAS DAY

'I have to go!' In a daze of happiness, Nell looked for a way down, her heart expanding like a balloon. She was full of fluttering nerves.

'You did it, Nell!' said Poco, giving her a big hug. 'All of it! Just by being you!'

The choir sang the song, Faith through smiles and tears of joy.

'Poco, thank you! You're the bravest numin that ever lived! She threw her arms around his neck. And you, Red!' She hugged him too. She grabbed Indy around his fuzzy neck and squeezed him tight. 'Thank you!' She grabbed the musicians one by one and held them close. 'All of you! Especially you!' She lifted Opus off his feet, who went crimson.

'Oh, ha ha! Steady!'

She waved at Ava on her perch, and at Glacia and Vaspar, who sat on a branch high above, their legs dangling. They gave Nell a little wave and continued watching the humans in the square. Ruby showered Nell in rainbow sparks and kissed her all over. Nell laughed.

Emma's mother was handing out little bags of birdseed. She couldn't think why Emma had suggested they bring it, and nor could Emma.

"Just a funny feeling," Emma had said. The scent of hot chocolate and mulled wine mingled with the sweet mist from the roasted honey chestnuts and marshmallows. Children laughed, throwing seeds to the crows, who danced and swooped for them. The humans brought boxes of beautifully wrapped presents to leave under the tree for strangers and friends to collect. Some were bright and colourful, with enormous bows on top. Others were wrapped in newspaper and tied up with string. One was in the shape of a bike. Two real sausage dogs wearing red bandanas weaved in and out of the human's legs and sniffed each other's bottoms. A little girl and boy had taken the pompom snowman and penguin off the tree and danced around with them, squashing them close. Nell turned to her friends.

'I must go to Emma. Thank you, friends, goodbye!'

Vaspar stood up. 'Nell, you must return for the procession tonight!'

'What procession?'

'It's Christmas Day! We must celebrate! The

fellowship lives and breathes! For us and our humans. Your version I mean. Not my terrible let's leave the human's plan. Phew, what a bad idea that was!' he rubbed his forehead. 'So embarrassing! We will call our version The Goodwill Fellowship, yes?'

'Yes!' They cheered.

'The Goodwill Fellowship,' said Opus, nodding as he conducted the choir singing All I want for Christmas.

'And look at us all! It will be a beautiful Christmas in Hope's End!' He flung his arms wide.

'Go,' Red said to Nell. 'I will fetch you a few minutes before midnight for the procession. I'll sort out the transport.' He winked. 'Meet you on the doorstep. What's the address?'

'25a Oakwood Road.' She hugged him again and looked for the fastest way down.

Red went back to showing Poco and others how to make a bow and arrow out of long pine needles.

'When this is over, come home with me if you like,' Indy said to him. 'There is plenty of room on my shelf, and my owner wouldn't notice. I think you would get on if he did.'

'I wouldn't hear of it,' said Nell as she dropped down. 'You must move in with us. Emma would love you.'

'Red, surely you will come home with us, back where you belong,' said Opus.

'I've got used to being a nomad.' He blushed. 'Perhaps I can take it in turns and visit you all?' They all nodded.

'Whatever you want, old chap,' said Opus, who

stretched up to pat Reds back. 'We all have to find our own way to be.'

'Besides, I have got rather friendly with the old man on the bench, Alfie.' He nodded out to him. 'He has a few challenges ahead I can help him with.' Alfie was eating mince pies with the woman from the boat. Ruby sparked lilac hearts when she saw her. Ava laughed.

'That's Ruby's owner, Rose,' she said. Nell smiled, and dangling from the branch with one hand, she waved.

'Goodbye friends, see you later!'

'Merry Christmas, Nell!' They cheered. Ruby buzzed over and pecked more kisses on her. Laughing, Nell dropped onto the branch below and made her way down.

＊

Fat clumps of snowflakes settled, leaving a carpet of glittering white. Mr Tribulus arrived in the square with the mayor carrying a huge pile of gifts to put under the tree. They spoke for a few minutes, his head hanging low. The mayor looked at the star on the tree top and scratched her head. A boy saw her looking and followed her gaze.

'My star!' said a boy. 'That's mine! At the top! I made that!' He pointed and jumped about. The crowd cheered and applauded him. His proud father, who had been roasting the chestnuts, was looking about him, enjoying the applause, too.

'My son!' he said, giving the boy a squeeze. 'My son made the star at the top!' The mayor smiled as if she had planned it all along and looked around for the angel. Two policewomen arrived and stood on either side of Mr Tribulus, who stared at his feet. The mayor, who was wearing an even larger jewelled collar than before, stood on a box and the people fell quiet. Straining under the weight of the collar, she began.

'Wonderful people of Hope's End! Thank you for your generous donations. We have given Christmas presents out to dozens of children and there are more here under our magnificent tree. Help yourselves! We raised thousands for local charities. The Holly Road foodbank is overflowing with Christmas gifts and treats! There is turkey and potatoes with stuffing and sausages in bacon, nut loaf, and everything else at the Grotto Social Centre for anyone who wants it!' Alfie and Rose jumped up from the bench and rushed towards the town together. 'Well done everyone!' said the mayor, clapping. The crowd cheered. 'And I have the best gift of all! You may have heard on the news this morning that we have discovered the cause of the illness! It's true! Now, we can heal the sick, starting today! We shall re-open the shops, the businesses, and get the town in order. Our lives will be back to normal before the year's end!' The crowds' cheers were deafening. 'And behold! Our magnificent Christmas tree! A beautiful creation we made together! This fine tree has reminded me, and I hope all of you, that we must stick together when life gets tough. Perhaps it even had something to do with solving our crisis who knows!' Laughter and applause went on for a long time. 'I was hoping there may be a gingerbread biscuit or two left, but it seems I'm too late!' A rounded crow on the railings burped up a small piece of red ribbon which looped down to the ground. 'I have never been so proud of this town.' She wiped away a tear. 'Oh, and if anyone sees my angel, please let me know. She was only from the car boot sale, but I rather liked her! Merry Christmas everyone!' She held her arms out wide.

'Merry Christmas!' they roared. A man spoke with Emma's mother. He was cheerful looking with a broad smile and plump cheeks. The numins looked out.

'I know him,' said Indy, staring out. 'He is friends with my owner, comes to the house sometimes.' Ava flapped closer and perched on a branch above.

'That's Bob from the bookshop. He will be thrilled the shop can open again.' Her eyes like little half-moons of joy. 'I need to take this back.' She held the stocking with the orb in her beak. 'No more stealing, Vaspar.'

'Never.' He crossed his heart. Ava flew off with the Christmas stocking, around the back of the yew hedge so as not to be seen, towards Church Street. It was heavy, but she was strong.

A man arrived on a motorbike and pulled up near Emma and her mother. He took off his helmet and a mop of red hair tumbled out. 'There is Joe, my owner!' said Indy. 'Wow, he bought another

motorbike. I never thought I would see the day.'
Two boys raced after him, shouting at him to give
them a ride on it. Joe hugged Bob and Emma's
mother and they chatted while the boys admired the
bike. 'And his nephews are staying!' said Indy, his
chocolate brown eyes sparkling. The worn patches
on his coat seemed smaller, almost gone.

'Like I said, our humans grow as we do,' said
Opus. 'He has re-kindled his adventurous spirit, like
you, Ha!' He slapped Indy's leg. Indy laughed.

Nell tucked a chocolate coin they had missed
when foraging under her arm for Emma. There was
now enough snow for snowballs, and Emma was
playing with the other children in a snowball fight.
Her cheeks were pink, and she had left her red coat
on the corner of a bench. Nell slid down a silver
ribbon and landed on the ground under the tree. She
looked for the best way to get all the way across the
square to Emma's coat pocket without being seen.
Just then, she heard banging and spluttering behind
her. It was the pixies in their Red Baron car. Nell
rolled her eyes.

'Oh, it's you,' she said. 'Great.' On top of the car
was the little gold bag that had bitten her on the tree.
'Even better.' She put her hands on her hips. The
pixies ignored her. One got out and reached inside
the bag and pulled out a fine powder. He threw it
over themselves and the car, and they vanished. Nell
scratched her head. Then, a shower of powder
drifted over her. When she looked down, she
couldn't see herself.

'Hey, that's great! Thanks!' The pixies drove

closer to her and knocked her into the car.

'Ow!'

'Well, do you want to get there or not? Hurry! It only lasts for one minute,' said the taller pixie.

The car sped across the square, the wind whizzing past Nell's ears. The pixies weaved the Red Baron between the humans' feet, then underneath the tummy of a sausage dog. They dashed through the falling snow all the way to Emma's coat. Nell didn't know whether to laugh or cry as they swerved about and skidded to a halt, sending her tumbling into a pile of snow.

'Thank you, I think!' She waved towards the two tiny wheel tracks appearing in the snow as they drove back to the tree. She brushed the snow from her body and climbed up Emma's coat, nestling herself back inside the pocket. 'See you tonight,' she whispered across the square to her friends on the tree, even though no one could hear. A glow of happiness crept from her heart across her whole body. She wrapped her arms around herself as the police took Mr Tribulus away to the station.

The Christmas tree winked and blinked through the white confetti-snow. The decorations twirled in the breeze as if nothing had happened. It was the most beautiful Christmas tree anyone had ever seen. She sighed, and peeked out of the pocket, fizzing with joy at the sight of Emma, who laughed with Joe's nephews and the other children.

'Mission accomplished!'

Emma's mother came over and put her arm around Emma. They stepped over the snow speckled cobbles towards the coat. Nell ducked back inside the pocket with the chocolate coin. Emma put her coat on, chattering to her mother. They walked towards home; Nell stowed in the pocket, brimming with happiness.

'Well, it looks like it will be a lovely Christmas after all! Dad will be home soon, and we can visit him right now. The turkey is in the oven, and we have roast potatoes and sausages wrapped in bacon, stuffing, lots of gravy, cranberry sauce, and sprouts of course.'

'It seems strange to eat a sprout,' said Emma.

'What else would you do with it?' said Emma's mother. 'Anyway, Bob from the bookshop is coming for lunch. Joe and his nephews are coming. It's going to be fun! And he baked a delicious chocolate Yule Log.'

'Oh good. So, yule not make me eat that disgusting Christmas pudding!' laughed Emma.

'Hey, it's tasty!' said her mother.

Emma peered into her breast pocket, a smudge of hot chocolate on her lip. Her eyes grew wide.

'Mum, what's this?' Her hand reached in. Nell felt Emma's gloved fingers close around her. She pulled her out. 'Mum! It's Nell!' She squeezed her under her chin.

'She must have been in there all along!' said her mother. 'I knew you would find her. Things don't just walk off by themselves, you know!'

'She wasn't there! I looked, loads of times, I swear.' Emma's mother smiled down at Emma, shaking her head. Emma's eyes lit up. 'Mum! I bet she has been on that Christmas tree making my wish come true all this time. Thank you, Nell. Merry Christmas!' She squeezed her even tighter and kissed her on the head. Nell fizzled with happiness.

'Really, darling. You do have a vivid imagination!'

Emma put Nell back in her pocket and pulled out the chocolate coin. 'She must have got me this!' she said. 'Thanks, Nell!' Emma's mother ruffled her hair as Emma opened her chocolate. Nell lay in her cosy pocket, bursting with love, the starlight tingling brighter than ever inside.

CHAPTER 29

THE GOODWILL FELLOWSHIP PARTY

At five minutes to midnight, Emma's hand clutched Nell's tiny body on her pillow. Nell's rosy cheeks ached; she was smiling so much. Though it always surprised her how loudly Emma could snore. Now, she had a party to get to. She prised herself out of Emma's fingers, trying not to wake her.

'See you in a few hours,' she whispered. Nell leapt from the bed and ran across the floor, down the hall. The air still smelt of leftover roast dinner and gingerbread. She pushed open the letterbox and she tumbled out onto the cold, hard ground. 'Ow!' She dusted herself off. On the pavement in front of her sat Red, waving from the back of a crow. Nell blinked. They grinned at each other.

'Hop on!' He beckoned her over. 'We don't want Colin to turn into a pumpkin!'

'You must be joking!' she said, her hands on her hips. Colin cawed.

'Don't be mean, or he won't want to bring you home after!' Red laughed. Poco poked his head around from behind Red.

'Come on, Nell, or we will miss it!' he said.

'Hello Poco. This is right up your street, isn't it!' Nell jumped on. Poco grinned as Colin ran forwards while the three friends clasped on to his feathers. He took off and glided through the icy air, the wind rushing past them. Snow had left its white cloak across the ground. Snowflakes splatted against their faces as they flew above gardens and the frozen pond. The fox Nell had met a few nights before looked up at them, scratching his head. She waved at him. They flew over Church Street and the bookshop where Bob was still up, carrying boxes back into the shop. Joe carried a pile of books, his motorbike propped up nearby. The men waved goodbye to Alfie and Rose, who were walking back to Riverside Square after helping them unload. Bob stooped down onto the doorstep and picked up a tiny Christmas stocking left there. He looked inside and saw something that looked rather like a marble. He looked up and down the street and shrugged. Colin flew on and swerved through the gap in the yew hedge and across the square to the Christmas tree. Nell held on tight, her pigtails swinging about behind her. The other numins were gathered for the procession. Nell's heart leapt into her throat as they swooped closer.

'Aim for a soft part, Coliiiin!' He tipped Nell, Red and Poco onto a branch where they tumbled flat on their faces near where the musicians, Indy and the others stood. They grabbed onto the needles while it bounced back into place. Colin flapped off to his friends on the railings.

'Woohoo!' They giggled.

'You're making a habit of dramatic entrances, Nell, ha!' Opus said. Indy and Ava laughed. Ruby spluttered white sparks like snow everywhere. Groups of numins chatted and joked together up and down the tree. The choir practiced their singing, ready for the procession. The golden violin joined in, with two wind-up music boxes.

'A Goodwill Fellowship for a hopeful town!' shouted Vaspar from the next branch. 'Let us take an oath! A dedication to helping each other, and our humans for as long as we are needed.'

'Oh, yes, yes,' said Opus, clapping his hands. 'Hmmm, something like "We, the numins of the Goodwill Fellowship, will live to help each other and the humans, for as long as we can." Will that do?'

'It's a little long, Opus, but yes, something like that. Repeat it everyone!' Nell and the others put their hands, hooves, or wings if they had them to their chest and spoke together.

'We, the numins of the Goodwill Fellowship, live to help each other and the humans for as long as we can.' They vowed. They each said slightly different words, but they all had the gist. The words spread through the numins all around the tree. Mick took a deep breath in and spluttered letters onto the breeze with the oath written on. The letters found their way into the nearby homes with more numins busy with their secret work. Like a whisper rippling through the streets, the words spread from numin to numin. A brass mermaid doorknocker on a front door on Crown Road sounded out. It alerted a keyring of a fuzzy kitten in a house around the corner to the oath. She trotted along Ferry Road and passed the oath on to a cuckoo clock hanging in the Barmy Arms Pub. The cuckoo flew off and spread the word further, and the oath rippled across the whole country. Ornaments and pens, old brooches and keys, paintings and rings, carvings, and toys, each passing the message on in their own way. The numin on the tree looked at each other warmly, Nell's chest filled with pride.

'Well! There is no time like the present!' said Opus. 'Let the procession begin! Nell, you at the front!' Nell tried to hide behind Indy.

'I insist!' Vaspar pulled her out and pushed her forward. She stepped in front of him, pulling Poco, Indy and Red along with her with a shy smile, and beckoned to the choir to follow. Ava perched on Indy's antler. Ruby looped above them, showering a golden spray of sparks over them. Glacia applauded, and everyone cheered.

'Alright, this way, everyone!' said Nell.

The numins danced their way around the tree, the choir singing Rocking Around The Christmas Tree. Bells wobbled and shook in time to the song. Ava rang her bell, and a little green drum added a beat.

They knocked into the baubles sending them spinning and rocking. Moon-kissed snowflakes landed on the snowy branches that glinted in the moonlight. The crows joined in, swooping around the tree in time to the music. The procession spread across the entire tree. The pixies drove the Red Baron, beeping and throwing little snowballs at everyone. The sheep formed a Conga and skipped along behind, with the donkey who carried a snoozing Ziggy on his back, followed by the guinea fowl, the cat, and the elephant. The dolphin shot out of the lower branches and over them, diving back into the knots of pine needles. Baubles seemed to take on the numin energy and bounced up and down. The tinsel, ribbon, and garlands formed Mexican waves rising and falling together around the tree. The toadstool leapfrogged over everyone. Mick the post box, Otto the nutcracker, and Anka the polar bear bookmark bopped along with Kevin the hare, heading Sprout to each other, who was crying with laughter.

'Again!' she shouted, over and over. The sausage dogs had made skis out of pine needles and raced on the snowy branches with the mice. The lizard took three tiny penguins on her back and slid behind them like a sleigh. The angry Santa was wiggling his hips, being followed around by the glass dragonfly, who chanted curious sounds to him. He shimmied over to Nell and cleared his throat.

'In case you were wondering, I am not actually the real Father Christmas.' She held in a laugh.

'Oh, really,' said Nell, 'I would never have

guessed!'

'Humph,' he said, and shimmied off. The numins fell around laughing. Suddenly, something hurtled out of the air and smacked Indy right on the head. His other lost antler pinged into place and fused into the fur as if it had always been there.

'How did that get there?' said Nell. Indy laughed, patting it with his hoof.

'Goodness, I lost that in Africa years ago. It must have travelled all the way back after our mending session. It was a long way away!' They looked over to Ziggy and the pompom snowman and clapped. 'Thank you again!' Indy bowed low to them.

Vaspar and Glacia danced under a piece of mistletoe, blushing. Nell, Red, and Poco covered their eyes. When Indy passed the mistletoe, the llama with colourful tassels leant over and gave him a kiss on the cheek. His chocolate drop eyes flashed. The large gold paper mâché star wheeled in circles at the top. Baubles, wreaths, mini-Christmas stockings, and little Christmas jumpers bounced along. Nell's heart shone. She waved ahead to Poco, who waved back.

'We don't need an angel when we have each other!' he yelled.

'Three cheers for the Goodwill Fellowship!' shouted Opus.

'Hip hip, hooray! Hip hip, hooray! Hip hip, hooray!'

The river boats knocked together in harmony. Alfie and Rose sat on the bench drinking mulled wine from cups with yet another batch of homemade mince pies. Neither were hungry after their enormous lunch in the town, but they stuffed them in, anyway. Both wore huge, new warm coats and admired the tree while they chatted. The tree appeared to spin like a merry-go-round. They shook their heads in disbelief, looking from the tree to the cups of mulled wine and back again. Scratching their heads, they burst into laughter. The pair got up and danced in the square, mulled wine spilling all over the place.

Snow cast a clean blanket of white across the town, the square and the branches of the great Christmas tree. Feathery silver moonbeams shone onto Nell and the Goodwill Fellowship of Hope's End while they danced together until the light of the new dawn.

The End

ABOUT THE AUTHOR

Whilst growing up I dreamt of tiny, friendly people secretly living alongside us humans. Writing *The Wish That Saved Christmas* made my imaginings a reality! I live in Twickenham, England, also known as Hope's End, with my nearly grown-up daughter and my sausage dog. Who knows; perhaps there may be a numin hiding here somewhere too.

I hope you enjoyed reading this as much as I enjoyed writing it. If so, please leave a review, this really helps indie authors.

Also available as an audiobook and e-book.

www.kate-harvey.co.uk

ACKNOWLEDGMENTS

With thanks to everyone at The Novelry, especially Louise Dean and her fabulous writing courses. I had invaluable support from Tash Barsby, Lily London, and Polly Ho Yen. Thanks to my readers Verity McLellan, Alex Webber, Grace Gilbert, Anna Atkin, and my mother.

Special thanks to Grace, who had to think about Christmas all year round for a really long time.

Printed in Great Britain
by Amazon